DEADLY DESTINY

Wolf Who Hunts Smiling lunged. Touch the Sky pivoted hard to his right and felt his enemy's blade nick the leather band around his left wrist as it passed harmlessly by. Touch the Sky leaped on top of the small but powerful Cheyenne and wrestled him to the ground.

"Stop!" Arrow Keeper shouted. "I forbid this fighting. I will not let you dirty the entire tribe."

"But, Father," Wolf Who Hunts Smiling said, "he—"

"Silence! Return to your clan circle."

After Wolf Who Hunts Smiling had departed, his face a mask of hatred for his enemy, Touch the Sky started to leave. But Arrow Keeper called his name.

"Yes, Father?"

"I have had a medicine dream. The vision tells me you will die soon!"

CHEYENNE

4

VISION QUEST
JUDD COLE

LEISURE BOOKS **NEW YORK CITY**

A LEISURE BOOK®

March 1993

Published by

Dorchester Publishing Co., Inc.
276 Fifth Avenue
New York, NY 10001

Printed in the United States of America.

Prologue

Ambushed by Bluecoat pony soldiers near the North Platte River, Running Antelope and his band of 30 Cheyenne braves fought with reckless courage. But they were not painted and dressed for battle—nor were their arrows and lances any match for the soldiers' carbines and artillery.

The lone survivor of the massacre was Running Antelope's infant son. The child was taken back to the river-bend settlement of Bighorn Falls in the Wyoming Territory. His Cheyenne name had been lost forever. He was renamed Matthew and raised by John and Sarah Hanchon, owners of the town's mercantile store.

In 1856, when Matthew turned 16, tragedy struck: He fell in love with Kristen, daughter of Hiram Steele, the wealthiest man in Bighorn Falls. Caught in their secret meeting-place, Matthew was viciously beaten by one of Steele's wranglers. And Kristen's

Judd Cole

suitor from nearby Fort Bates, a jealous young cavalry officer named Seth Carlson, threatened to ruin John Hanchon's all-important contract with the fort unless Matthew cleared out for good.

Thus driven from the only world he knew, the youth rode north to the up-country of the Powder River, Cheyenne country, seeking the people whose blood he shared. Captured by Cheyenne braves from Chief Yellow Bear's camp, he was accused of being a spy for the whites.

Only the intervention of old Arrow Keeper, the tribal medicine man, saved him from death by torture. The elder had recognized the birthmark, buried past the youth's hairline, from a medicine vision: a mulberry-colored arrowhead, the mark of the warrior. This tall youth was destined to lead his people in a final, great victory against their enemies.

Renamed Touch the Sky by Arrow Keeper, the unwelcome arrival was hated by Black Elk and his bitter young cousin Wolf Who Hunts Smiling. Black Elk was furious with jealousy when Chief Yellow Bear's daughter, Honey Eater, made love talk with Touch the Sky instead of him. And Wolf Who Hunts Smiling symbolically announced his intention to kill the suspected spy, walking between Touch the Sky and the campfire.

Even after Touch the Sky and his white friend Corey Robinson saved the Cheyenne village from annihilation by Pawnees he was not fully accepted as a warrior. Then whiskey traders invaded Indian country, led by the ruthless Henri Lagace.

Not only did the whiskey peddlers threaten to destroy the Indian way of life with their strong water. Lagace and his men had taken to slaughtering white trappers in their sleep, making the murders look like Cheyenne handiwork. Thus they profited when the panicked Territorial Commission declared a bounty on the scalp of any Cheyenne.

Lagace kidnapped Yellow Bear's daughter and threatened to kill her if the Cheyenne went on the warpath against him. But Yellow Bear could not sacrifice his tribe to save Honey Eater. The only hope was to send a small Cheyenne war party, led by Black Elk, into the heavily fortified white stronghold.

Touch the Sky was told, in a medicine vision, that he must defy Black Elk or Honey Eater would die. He deserted the war party and infiltrated the white camp on his own. He was taken prisoner and brutally tortured. But his courage rallied the other Cheyenne to mount an heroic surprise assault.

They scattered the white devils and freed Honey Eater. Touch the Sky then pursued his enemy Lagace until he killed him, ending the scalps-for-bounty menace. But much of his valor went unwitnessed, and many in the tribe were still unconvinced of his loyalty.

Their suspicions only deepened when Touch the Sky's friend Corey Robinson arrived at Yellow Bear's camp with bad news for the young Cheyenne: Hiram Steele had conspired, with Lieutenant Seth Carlson, to take over John and Sarah Hanchon's mercantile store. Now the two had launched a campaign to drive the Hanchons from their mustang spread.

Touch the Sky, badly needed by the tribe and Honey Eater because Chief Yellow Bear lay dying,

Judd Cole

was torn in his loyalties. Tribal law would not permit Honey Eater to live alone if her father died—
meaning she would have to accept Black Elk's
brideprice. But in the end he realized his white parents' battle was his battle. He returned to Bighorn
Falls accompanied by his friend, the battle-hardened
young warrior Little Horse.

They defeated their white enemies, but a new
battle raged for Touch the Sky, a battle in his
heart: Returning to Bighorn Falls crossed his trail
with Kristen's. Seeing her again rekindled his pas-
sion and left him hopelessly trapped between two
worlds, at home in neither.

Nor did he and Little Horse realize, as they started
back to Yellow Bear's camp on the Powder River,
the trouble which awaited them. Spies had watched
them during their battle, mistaking Touch the Sky's
meetings with the sympathetic cavalry officer Tom
Riley as proof the Cheyenne was a traitor to his
people.

Chapter One

"Brother," said Little Horse, breaking the long silence of their ride, "I am glad to return to Cheyenne hunting grounds. But during our absence I fear our people may have turned their hearts to stone against us."

Touch the Sky, easily the taller of the two young Cheyenne, nodded his agreement. Both youths had halted their ponies side by side on the rim of a long, grassy slope which formed the east wall of the Powder River valley. Below, a huge fork marked where the Little Powder joined the Powder.

Touch the Sky lifted one sun-bronzed arm to point at the tipis far below them. They were arranged in clan circles beside the fork, casting long shadows now that their sister, the sun, was nearing her resting place. Down near the water, a group of naked children were throwing stones at birds. Squaws knelt beside the tripods out-

9

side their tipi entrances, cooking elk and buffalo meat.

"At least," replied Touch the Sky, "all appears well below."

Both Cheyenne youths understood his unstated meaning: *At least the tribe was not slaughtered while we deserted them to fight white men's battles.*

"Once the Councillors learn who we defeated," said Little Horse, "perhaps the tribe will think differently."

"Perhaps," said Touch the Sky, though doubt was clear in his tone. "But will they believe us when we tell them that the paleface devils who tried to destroy my white parents were among those who rode with the scar-faced whiskey trader, Lagace?"

Little Horse was silent at this, knowing they had nothing but their word to prove their claim. In the eyes of the tribe, they had deserted their people when Chief Yellow Bear was sick—a vulnerable time for attack by enemies.

They nudged their ponies' flanks with their knees, descending closer to Yellow Bear's village. With each step nearer, Touch the Sky felt invisible flies stirring in his belly. His eyes swept the camp constantly as he tried to spot Honey Eater.

Was her father better now, or had Arrow Keeper's strong medicine failed to cure him? Had their chief crossed over to the Land of Ghosts? Did Honey Eater too believe he had deserted his people? All these questions cankered at him as the two youths descended the long slope.

Touch the Sky was lean and straight, tall even

for a Cheyenne. He had a strong, hawk nose and jet-black locks cut close over his eyes to keep his vision clear. The warm moons were upon them now, with the new grass well up—both youths were bare to the waist and wore beaded buckskin leggings, elkskin moccasins, and soft doeskin breechclouts. Leather bands around their left wrists protected them from the hard slap of their buffalo-sinew bowstrings.

"Brother!" said Little Horse when they had covered perhaps half the distance to the camp. "Look!"

He pointed to the lone hummock, between the river and the rest of the clan circles, which was reserved for the chief's tipi. An old Cheyenne sat outside the entrance flap, smoking a clay pipe and watching the children play. The elder had long gray hair streaked with white and his face was a seamed mass of deep wrinkles, though still hatchet-sharp in profile.

But it wasn't the face of Chief Yellow Bear. It was Arrow Keeper, the tribal medicine man.

"Our chief has crossed over while we were gone," said Little Horse with conviction. "This can mean nothing else. Yellow Bear's tipi has been taken down and placed on his scaffold with him. Arrow Keeper is our new chief!"

Suddenly, one of the sentries hidden in the trees circling camp raised the wolf howl of alarm.

The two Cheyenne bucks stared at each other, realizing they had just been spotted—and that the wolf howl was always reserved for announcing the arrival of enemies!

Even before they could nudge their ponies into motion again, a group of warriors rode hard from

11

camp to meet them. Now the crier was racing up and down through camp on his pony, announcing their arrival.

The fierce young war chief named Black Elk led the warriors. He was accompanied by his younger cousin Wolf Who Hunts Smiling. When they reached the two arrivals, they formed a circle around them with lances raised.

"The white men's spies have come back like dogs returning to their vomit," said Wolf Who Hunts Smiling. "They are the eyes and ears of the Bluecoats!"

Touch the Sky locked stares with his sworn enemy. Wolf Who Hunts Smiling was small but hard-knit, with a guarded, wily face and furtive dark eyes that missed nothing. Ever since his capture, Wolf Who Hunts Smiling had accused him of being a spy. And one night he had deliberately stepped between Touch the Sky and the campfire—the Cheyenne way of announcing one's intention of killing another.

"I have no ears for your lies," said Touch the Sky. "Words are cheap, the coins spent freely by gossiping old squaws. Where is the proof that I or Little Horse have played the white men's dogs?"

"*There* is the proof!" said Wolf Who Hunts Smiling, pointing toward the braves named River of Winds and Swift Canoe. "They were sent to spy on you. They saw you making big medicine with the Bluecoat war chief! They saw you make war against paleface settlers so that Cheyennes would be blamed for the attacks!"

"You speak in a wolf bark!" said Touch the Sky. But he and Little Horse exchanged shocked glances as they realized the horrible mistake the tribe was making.

"The Bluecoat we made medicine with is a friend to the red man," said Little Horse. "He was—"

"Silence!" commanded Black Elk, speaking for the first time since the party had circled them.

Black Elk had seen only 20 winters, but already his war bonnet was filled with the eagle feathers of bravery. He was big and, unlike many red men, heavily muscled. His fierce black eyes were made even more fierce by the partially torn-off ear which he had sewn back onto his own skull with buckskin thread. His hair, like that of the others, had been cropped off short in mourning for Chief Yellow Bear.

"You say my cousin speaks in a wolf bark," he said to Touch the Sky. "But *I* speak only the straight word. The Headmen have not yet voted against you, so I will not take you prisoner. Though the tribe is angry at Little Horse, this is his home. But *you* are not welcome here! Before you ride closer, surrender your rifle!"

Hot blood stippled his cheeks, but Touch the Sky obeyed. He slid the percussion-action Sharps, a present from his white father in Bighorn Falls, out of the buckskin scabbard he had sewn to his blanket. He handed it to Black Elk.

"If this is my home," said Little Horse, "it is also Touch the Sky's home. If he is not welcome, I am not welcome."

"Speak carefully, your place here is not assured," said Black Elk. "If you desire it, perhaps you can join your brother when he is banned from Cheyenne lands forever!"

Touch the Sky and Little Horse were both silent as they were escorted the rest of the way down to the camp. Black Elk's ominous words had evoked the memory of something old Arrow Keeper had once told them: *A Cheyenne without a tribe is a dead man.*

The hostile stares and accusing faces of the others, as they rode in, stirred unpleasant memories for Touch the Sky: memories of that day when, beaten and lashed to a travois, he had first been brought to camp as a prisoner and suspected spy.

His present misery still wasn't complete, however, until he caught his first glimpse of Honey Eater.

Again, just as he had when he was still called Matthew Hanchon and saw her for the first time, he was struck by her frail beauty—the high, finely sculpted cheekbones, the long, black hair braided with white petals of mountain columbine.

But it wasn't the mere sight of Honey Eater that made Touch the Sky's heart constrict in agony. It was the fact that, as she met his eyes, she was staring past the flap of Black Elk's tipi— and she was wearing the beaded bride-shawl of a newlywed!

Two sleeps passed, though in his misery Touch the Sky hardly noticed whether moon or sun owned the sky.

Out of respect for Yellow Bear, he and Little Horse had cropped their hair short like the other warriors. But Touch the Sky made no further attempt to join tribal life, nor was he welcome to.

He kept to his tipi by night, spent most of his days in the huge rope corrals working his ponies—the same ponies he had hoped to offer as the bride-price for Honey Eater. Only Little Horse was friendly to him. Arrow Keeper seemed to be avoiding him.

He knew that the Councillors would soon meet to decide his fate. But curiously, in his sorrow he was indifferent to his future. Let the Headmen vote with their stones to kill him, banish him, it was all one to him.

The others ignored him, looking right through him as if he were *odjib*—a thing of smoke. The report by River of Winds carried much weight. His word was well respected, and he had a reputation for fairness.

Tragically, the meetings he had witnessed between the Bluecoat pony soldier Tom Riley and Touch the Sky were not what they appeared to be. The officer had secretly joined forces with the Cheyenne to help them fool the paleface army. But Touch the Sky knew he could never prove this.

True, returning to Bighorn Falls and seeing Kristen Steele again had rekindled the dormant feelings in his heart for her. Seeing her had once again plunged him into a crisis—was he a white man, a red man, or an eternal outsider? Then, that first sight of Honey Eater, upon his return, had convinced him he loved the Cheyenne maiden too.

She had once crossed her wrists over her heart for him—Indian sign talk for love. Now she was Black Elk's wife!

On the third night after his return, Touch the Sky was walking back to his tipi after bathing in the river. A familiar voice called to him out of the grainy twilight.

"Woman Face!"

Touch the Sky drew up short. He was near the center of camp, nearly deserted now as most of the tribe prepared their late meal. The hide-covered frame of the council lodge loomed out of the darkness like a still, shaggy buffalo.

Only Wolf Who Hunts Smiling still called him Woman Face—a mocking reference to his old white man's habit of letting his emotions show in his face.

"So? Have you finally decided to make good on your threat to put me under?" said Touch the Sky. "Best to look before you wade in further—your cousin has my rifle, but he did not take my knife."

"Why should I risk dirtying the Sacred Arrows by shedding your blood now?" said Wolf Who Hunts Smiling. "The Headmen meet tomorrow to discuss you. Thanks to River of Winds' report, you will either be killed or banished. Either way, I am satisfied."

So his fate would be settled tomorrow? He was ready.

"Yes, you are satisfied," said Touch the Sky. "Just as a filthy pig is satisfied to eat its own droppings."

"Brave talk, Woman Face. But perhaps if you were more of a man your sweet Honey Eater would not be lying naked right now with my cousin!"

Hot rage surged into his face. Touch the Sky reached for the obsidian knife in his sheath.

"Sing the Death Song, Cheyenne," said Touch

the Sky softly as he drew his blade, "then draw your knife. If I am to be banished or killed, let me earn my punishment now!"

In a moment Wolf Who Hunts Smiling's bone-handle knife was in his hand. "As you will, white man's dog! Tonight one of us crosses over!"

Wolf Who Hunts Smiling lunged. Touch the Sky pivoted hard to his right and felt his enemy's blade nick the leather band around his left wrist as it passed harmlessly by. Touch the Sky leaped on top of the small but powerful Cheyenne and wrestled him to the ground.

Wolf Who Hunts Smiling wriggled free, rose to his feet, raised his knife, and prepared to leap again.

"Stop!"

Both youths glanced toward the speaker, bare-ly discernible in the faltering light.

Arrow Keeper!

"Listen to your chief, young Cheyenne bucks! I speak words I want you to carry away with you. I forbid this fighting. Have we not enough enemies outside the tribe trying to kill us? I am still the keeper of the sacred Medicine Arrows. Any Cheyenne blood shed by another Cheyenne stains the Arrows. I will not let you dirty the entire tribe!"

"But, Father," Wolf Who Hunts Smiling said, "he—"

"Silence! Return to your clan circle."

After Wolf Who Hunts Smiling had departed, his face a mask of hatred for his enemy, Touch the Sky sheathed his knife and likewise started to leave. But Arrow Keeper called his name. He turned around.

17

"Yes, Father?"

"Return with me to my tipi, I would speak with you about urgent matters. I have had a medicine dream. The vision tells me you will die soon!"

Chapter Two

"You will die soon," repeated Arrow Keeper, "unless you leave before the Councillors decide your fate."

They sat in the gathering darkness just outside the entrance of Arrow Keeper's tipi. The acting chief struck fire from a piece of flint with his knife, igniting a small pile of bark-and-twig kindling. Flames leaped up, highlighting the seams and ridges of Arrow Keeper's face and the youthful sculpting of Touch the Sky's.

"The chief-renewal finally draws near," said Arrow Keeper. "The scattered bands of Cheyenne have nearly all returned to our valley for the ceremony. Soon there will be a time of dancing, feasting, and gift-giving. The tribe will name a successor now that our chief has been summoned."

Arrow Keeper automatically made the cut-off sign, as one did when speaking of the dead. Nor did he pronounce Yellow Bear's name aloud—the dead might hear their name and speak back.

"Soon I will no longer be chief. Then your only friend besides me will be Little Horse. And some in the tribe have already turned their hearts to stone against him for befriending you.

"So what will you do, little brother? My power to protect you will be limited. True it is, I am the Keeper of the Arrows. For this important responsibility I am respected. But the younger warriors, those who gather about Wolf Who Hunts Smiling and Swift Canoe and some of the others, are speaking more openly against me. And against you."

Arrow Keeper nudged the end of a log into the growing fire. Then he said, "A medicine dream, two sleeps ago, told me that you must die if the Council is allowed to meet and vote with their stones. Many in the tribe have spoken. They will not feel safe if a Bluecoat spy is alive among us."

Touch the Sky's mouth was a grim, determined slit in the flickering light. "Do *you* believe I am a Bluecoat spy, Father?"

"How would you ask me this thing? Did I not watch you save our chief's life by killing the Pawnee dog, War Thunder, with your battle ax? Did you not descend into the belly of the beast to save Honey Eater from the white devils who sold strong water? I have always talked only one way to you, and I say this. You are a true Cheyenne warrior, one worthy to wear the medicine hat in battle!"

"Perhaps," said Touch the Sky, his voice bitter with betrayal. "But my bravery did not prevent Honey Eater from accepting Black Elk's bride-price."

"Little brother, she did not make this decision lightly. She came to me in agony, but what would you have me tell this good young woman who is now alone in the world? That she should forsake everything and wait for you, a suspected spy, and infuriate Black Elk and the rest of the tribe?

"It may not always be fair, but our law does not permit our young women such choices. She is Cheyenne and must follow the Cheyenne way. Even a stone goes on being a stone."

Touch the Sky knew these words rang true. But still he could not crush the bitter sense of betrayal, the knife-edged doubts about his own ability to ever be a Cheyenne.

Arrow Keeper, studying his face closely in the flickering light, read these thoughts.

"It is not just the vote of the Headmen which I fear," he told the younger Cheyenne. "It is your own misery and doubt about being a red man which must also be defeated. True death, for any Indian, is to be alone forever. This is why a red man would rather fall on his own knife than be hated by his tribe. In your heart you are alone, even when surrounded by others. You cannot go on this way, living in two worlds yet belonging to neither."

Touch the Sky nodded, knowing these words flew straight-arrow.

"But what can I do, Father? As you say, I am alone. Honey Eater is Black Elk's squaw. I have already asked too much of Little Horse."

"You are alone, yes. And for this very reason, I am sending you on an important mission in the name of the entire tribe."

21

Sudden curiosity muted the misery in Touch the Sky's face.

"A mission?"

"Yes. A vision quest. There will be no fatal council because you will be on a sojourn to sacred Medicine Lake, seeking a medicine dream of great consequence to the Cheyenne people. As acting chief, I have the power to order this thing."

"A vision quest," repeated Touch the Sky.

The old shaman nodded. "Yes. A journey to the center of the red man's world. You remember when I spoke words about the mark hidden in your hair?"

Touch the Sky nodded. In the hair over his left temple, buried past the hairline, was a mulberry-colored birthmark shaped like an arrowhead— the mark of the warrior.

"I have already spoken to you about the powerful vision I experienced at Medicine Lake. But now I understand that *you* too must seek the same vision. If the hand of Maiyun, the Supernatural, is truly in this thing, then He will send the vision to you too."

Touch the Sky was silent, listening to the wood hiss and spit as the flames devoured it. He recalled well the vision Arrow Keeper had once described to him.

The elder had spent three grueling days in the Black Hills, standing in cold lake water up to his neck while he stared into the sun. On the third day the vision came.

It was a powerful dream, much of its meaning revealed in symbols, yet much of it also painfully clear. The vision had shown, in awful detail,

the suffering that was in store for the Cheyenne
people at the hands of paleface intruders. Soon,
during cold moons yet to come, the Cheyenne
would be forced to flee north to the Land of the
Grandmother, which the whites called Canada.

The wind would howl like mating wolves, the
temperature would fall so low the trees would
split open with sounds like gunshots. There
would be no wood for fires. The only way to
save some of the infants would be to slaughter ponies and remove some of the warm guts,
stuffing the little ones inside to keep them from
freezing. The elders would freeze with the Death
Song still on their lips.

But the vision also prophesized the rise of the
long-lost son of the great chief Running Antelope—a son who had been reported killed along
with his father and mother many winters ago.
This young warrior would gather his people from
all their far-flung hiding places and lead them in
one last, great victory for the Cheyennes.

"I believe this vision was a true vision," said
Arrow Keeper. "Not strong medicine placed over
my eyes by my enemies. I believe *you* are Running
Antelope's son—the arrowhead mark proves this.

"But it is not enough that *I* have seen this
vision. Just as one man cannot eat or drink or
hold a girl in his blanket for another, he cannot inspire another with his private visions. *You*
must experience the vision in all of its force at
Medicine Lake. Only then can you resolve this
terrible battle in your heart. Only then will you
accept who you are and what must be done."

Touch the Sky thought about all of this for a
long while. Arrow Keeper was right about the

terrible battle in his heart. But though he trusted and respected the old warrior greatly, Touch the Sky could not believe that *he* was the young war leader of Arrow Keeper's vision. Surely it was Black Elk.

Touch the Sky finally nodded. "When must I leave?"

"Immediately. Before the sun begins her next journey across the sky. You must purify yourself in the sweat lodge before you leave and again when you arrive. I will announce at the Council that I have sent you on this mission to seek spiritual guidance for the tribe. Many will not be happy, but I have ordered the sentries to let you ride out."

"But Father, what if I fail in seeking this medicine dream?"

Arrow Keeper stared long into the fire. When he finally answered, his voice was surprisingly sad and gentle.

"Before you entered the whiskey traders' camp, did you not experience a powerful vision? What man has done, man can do. But I will not coat the truth with honey. You will either experience this medicine vision, young Cheyenne warrior, or I fear you will be killed in the attempt."

Darkness settled like a heavy quilt over the Powder River village. The night sentries were posted, ready to raise the wolf howl if danger approached. Fires blazed throughout camp, and the young braves began gathering to gamble and bet on the pony races.

Touch the Sky heard the noise recede behind him as he descended the long grassy slope to the bank of the river. He veered toward the dark mass of an isolated hut built right next to the flowing water. It was made of buffalo hides stretched tight over a willow-branch frame.

Touch the Sky stooped, ducked inside, and started a fire to heat a circle of rocks. When they glowed hot, he stepped back outside and quickly stripped. Then he filled a wooden bowl with cold river water and poured it on the rocks.

The hot steam was difficult to breathe, at first. But soon, as rivulets of sweat began to pour from him, he felt his muscles relaxing. The confused stampede of his thoughts settled down to focus on one goal: the vision quest Arrow Keeper was sending him on. The old shaman insisted this vision would convince him of his place and purpose. Therefore, Touch the Sky desired it more than anything else.

Still, Arrow Keeper's words lingered in his memory like an echo: *You will either experience the medicine vision or be killed in the attempt.*

He finally emerged, rested and glistening with sweat in the moonlight, and rubbed his body down thoroughly with clumps of sage. Now it was time to make his preparations for the journey to Medicine Lake.

First he walked down river to the huge corral marked off by buffalo-hair ropes. He spotted his spirited dun grazing in the moonlight. But Touch the Sky knew she needed to rest and graze, to heal her scarred hocks and recover from the hard service she had given him lately.

Instead, he slipped his hackamore onto a spotted gray with a beautiful white mane. She was his trophy after counting first coup on a Crow warrior during a practice raid when Black Elk was training him. The pony was well trained, yet like all Cheyenne-trained horses had not been spirit-broken nor water-starved and beaten, as whites did to their horses. He led the gray back to his tipi and tethered her with a long strip of rawhide.

He slipped inside and gathered his few possessions. Black Elk had taken his rifle, leaving him with his knife, his stone-headed throwing-ax, his bow, and a foxskin quiver full of fire-hardened arrows.

He gathered extra moccasins, and stuffed his legging sash with pemmican and dried plums and jerked buffalo meat.

He skirted the activity in the middle of camp, sticking close to the river as he rode out. Not once did he look back. But his heart felt like a cold fist of stone in his chest, and he had never felt more alone in his life.

Thus distracted, his mind set fully on his purpose, he rounded a dense river thicket.

A lone figure glided out of the thick growth and into the pale-as-ice moonlight, startling him and making the gray shy in fright.

In a moment his knife was in his hand. He was about to slide from his pony and meet the attacker when he realized his "enemy" was Honey Eater!

Ever since Touch the Sky's return from the fight in Bighorn Falls, Honey Eater had been distraught with worry and remorse. In her heart she had never stopped loving him, and she had secretly been watching him since his return.

She knew he did not understand—in order to marry Black Elk, she had convinced herself that Touch the Sky had deserted her and the tribe. River of Winds' report had confirmed this, including the information that Touch the Sky was making love talk to a paleface girl with hair like spun-gold sunlight.

Only then had she finally married the importunate Black Elk. And now Touch the Sky was back, and Honey Eater knew she could love only him. Seeing him make preparations to leave, and at great risk of discovery, she had slipped off to meet him as he left.

Touch the Sky, however, could know none of this. His first thought, when he spotted Honey Eater, was that she had taken her nightly walk to gather fresh white columbine for her hair. He assumed the meeting was accidental, and his foremost desire was to get away—get away quickly before his own love and sense of betrayal forced him to break down in front of her.

"Touch the Sky!" she cried out behind him as he dug his knees into his pony and sprinted off into the blue-black darkness. But a moment later he was gone, disappearing like a wraith.

Honey Eater did not realize, as she stood weeping beside the bubbling river, that her brief meeting had been witnessed.

Wolf Who Hunts Smiling and Swift Canoe too had been watching Touch the Sky, aware that he was departing camp with Arrow Keeper's permission. But they rounded the thicket only in time to see their enemy bolt away, as if suddenly discovered. They were not soon enough to see that his meeting with Black Elk's bride was accidental.

"Brother," whispered Swift Canoe, who was crouched behind a hawthorn bush, "do you credit what your eyes behold? Your cousin's wife meeting secretly with Woman Face!"

Wolf Who Hunts Smiling's face, in the silvery moonlight, was furtive and calculating. "I have eyes to see, brother. And look now how she calls after him! She has sworn the squaw-taking vows with Black Elk, but now turns her stallion into a gelding!"

"Black Elk will beat her and cut off her nose when he learns of this," said Swift Canoe. "He may sing the Throw-away Song or even take her out on the plains."

Wolf Who Hunts Smiling nodded, though this last was rare and very extreme. The Throw-away Song was a public divorce. But taking a woman out on the plains was the worst punishment possible for an unfaithful Cheyenne woman: It meant that any warrior in the tribe who wanted to was free to lie with her. Afterward, polluted, she would be left to die alone and in shame.

"Come," said Wolf Who Hunts Smiling. "We must report this thing to my cousin. Black Elk's pride will do more than punish Honey Eater— he will *never* allow Touch the Sky to live after this!"

Chapter Three

Wolf Who Hunts Smiling and Swift Canoe were unable to report their news to Black Elk immediately.

On the previous day the hunters had run into exceptional luck near Sweet Medicine Creek, bringing down three full-grown elks and a fat mule deer. So much meat to butcher and pack in required help from camp. And friendly Sioux scouts had recently reported that Pawnee patrols had invaded Cheyenne country—meaning an armed war party would have to accompany the hunters back with their valuable haul.

Black Elk had led the war party. They had not returned until their uncle, the moon, had journeyed well across the sky. Wolf Who Hunts Smiling and Swift Canoe lingered about impatiently the next morning, until Honey Eater finally emerged from Black Elk's tipi and started the cooking fire.

Soon after, Black Elk emerged and ate his morning meal. Afterward, he moved to the shade behind his tipi and sat to file arrowpoints, which he had fastened onto a cottonwood stick to hold them. The two young warriors finally approached him.

"Cousin!" said Wolf Who Hunts Smiling.

Black Elk looked up. He was still tired, and his face still puffy and lopsided from sleep. Even so, the ear sewn back onto his skull with buckskin thread gave him a particularly fierce aspect.

"I would speak with you," said Wolf Who Hunts Smiling.

"You have a tongue," said Black Elk impatiently. "Use it."

Knowing a storm was about to break, Wolf Who Hunts Smiling glanced toward the tipi and lowered his voice. Then he announced bluntly, "Honey Eater has been meeting with Touch the Sky. He holds her in his blanket. We saw them last night."

Black Elk had expected nothing like this. For a moment his face was blank, the words too impossible to believe. Then, abruptly, hot blood rushed to his face.

"You speak in a wolf bark! Everyone knows you hate Touch the Sky. I care nothing for the trouble between you and your enemy, nor what lies you speak of each other. But now you claim that my bride has sullied the Medicine Arrows!

"Cousin! A moment before, I told you that you have a tongue. Now, I swear by Maiyun, I will cut it from your head!"

"I speak the straight word! Swift Canoe saw them too."

Swift Canoe bravely met Black Elk's fierce dark eyes and nodded.

"Both of you hate him!" said Black Elk. But desperation had crept into his tone. Adultery was a serious charge, as serious—and almost as rare among the Cheyenne—as the murder of a fellow Cheyenne. No one would make such a charge lightly.

Abruptly, Black Elk threw down the arrowpoints and stood up, hurrying into his tipi. The two youths expected a storm from within as Black Elk confronted his squaw. But instead he emerged a moment later, holding a curled piece of red willow bark.

"Swear this thing you have told me," he challenged them, thrusting forward the piece of bark. "Swear it on the Sacred Arrows!"

They glanced down and saw a red-clay drawing of the four Medicine Arrows, two pointing vertically, the other pair crossing them horizontally. No Cheyenne would lie while swearing on the Arrows, even on a symbolic drawing of them. Without hesitating, both bucks placed their hands on the bark and swore their oath.

Finally Black Elk believed them.

The hot, jealous rage which consumed him almost caused him to rush inside and kill Honey Eater on the spot. But following hard upon his rage came another emotion: shame. How could he, a proud warrior whose bonnet was full of coup feathers, admit to the tribe that his squaw was secretly meeting the outcast spy?

He could divorce his wife on the drum, of course. And this was a great disgrace for any squaw, let alone a chief's daughter. The men in the man's clan would sing the Throw-away Song while the husband danced by himself, holding a stick in his hand. Dancing up to the drum, the man hit it with his stick.

31

Boom! "I throw away my wife." With those words a warrior could drum his wife away, making a public quit-claim to all responsibility toward the squaw.

But the entire tribe would soon learn why. And never would he be respected—a war chief who could not keep his wife from rutting with a white man's dog! Besides—despite her treachery, Black Elk still loved Honey Eater. Better to pretend nothing had happened. Better to eliminate the other half of the problem.

Better, decided Black Elk, to kill Touch the Sky.

True, the mysterious stranger had the fighting spirit of a cougar and had developed into the best warrior Black Elk had ever trained. But he did not respect the Cheyenne way. He was a threat to the entire tribe, as this blackest of crimes proved.

Once again Black Elk held out the red willow bark.

"You have long thirsted for Touch the Sky's blood," Black Elk said to his cousin. "If you and Swift Canoe will make a vow of silence about this thing you have told me, I will give you my permission to kill him. And I will help you do it secretly, so the tribe will not know it was you."

The two friends readily agreed and swore their vow.

Arrow Keeper had already announced to the Councillors that Touch the Sky had been sent in the direction of the sun's birthplace on a vision quest at Medicine Lake.

"Pawnee are said to be in the area," said Black Elk. "I will announce to the others that, as War Chief, I have sent you two out on an important scouting mission. Ride hard toward the Black Hills and be waiting when this squaw-stealing dog arrives. Wash his white man's stink from our tribe forever. For the sake of our people, kill him, Cheyenne warriors!"

The Pawnee warrior named Red Plume halted the line of braves behind him by raising his streamered lance high over his head.

One by one, all six braves nudged their ponies up beside their leader's. From behind a huge pile of scree high up in the rimrock, they watched a lone rider below make his way slowly across the open tableland near the Powder River.

"Cheyenne," said a keen-eyed brave named Gun Powder, recognizing the distinctive red handprint on the pony's left forequarter.

Normally, at a distance, the distinctive cut of the hair was the quickest way to guess an Indian's tribe. But this youth had cropped short his hair in mourning, a practice common among several Plains tribes.

"We have been patient long enough," said Red Plume. "Yellow Bear has crossed over. The best time for a surprise attack will be during their chief-renewal, when all have assembled with their gifts for the poor. We need only wait until darkness, as we did when our people stole their Sacred Arrows. These white-livered Shaiyena fear the darkness."

Red Plume was referring to the great battle, many winters ago, when the Pawnee had captured the Cheyenne's Sacred Arrows. Though their enemy had eventually regained them, a hatred inspired by bloodlust had grown between the two tribes ever since.

The Pawnee, who called themselves Chahiksi-chakihs, "men of men," were naked save for clouts and elkskin moccasins. Bright red plumage adorned their greased topknots, which rose stiff and straight from otherwise shaved skulls. Their powerful bows, made from the wood of the Osage orange, were feared throughout Plains country.

"Our shadows grow long in the sun," said Gun Powder. "We have only to trail him until he makes his camp for the night."

In contrast to the Cheyenne and most other Plains Indians, the Pawnee liked to travel and attack after dark. Their priests taught that all energy derived from the stars and constellations. Therefore, the tribe possessed an extensive knowledge of the heavens and commonly employed star charts to move about freely at night. Other Plains Indians named the stars, but—fearing darkness—had not learned to navigate by them.

"No," said Red Plume. "We seize him now, in the open, before he possibly meets with others. And then we learn from him exactly when and where the chief-renewal will be. Until we know this thing, we cannot know the best time to bring in the main body for the attack."

Red Plume slid a stone-tipped arrow from his quiver and lined the notch up with the buffalo-sinew bowstring. The others followed suit.

Riding out of the blazing sun behind them to disguise their movement, the Pawnee descended from the high country with blood in their eyes.

His mind numb with sadness, Touch the Sky had ridden due east all day long, letting his pony set her own pace.

34

It would still be several more sleeps' ride before he would spot the rolling, dark-forested humps of the Black Hills on the horizon. Medicine Lake was nestled high among the hills. He had visited the sacred center of the Cheyenne world once before, when Arrow Keeper taught him the rudiments of Cheyenne customs and religion.

All that seemed as distant to him now as a long-forgotten dream. So much had happened since then: He had become a warrior, slain enemies, earned his first coup feather, withstood vicious torture—and sworn his eternal love to Honey Eater, who had returned his vow.

But everything he had done, like Honey Eater's love, was nothing but smoke behind him. He was hated as much by the tribe now as on the first day of his capture. For them, the white man's stink could never be washed from his skin, though it was red skin like theirs.

The spotted gray shied when a rabbit darted across their path, bringing Touch the Sky back to the present.

With a start of guilt, he glanced all around the sprawling vastness surrounding him. For a long time he had been riding with no attention to where he was going. The plains stretched out endlessly before him, the green and ochre colors bleeding together now as the sun neared her resting place. The river snaked its winding way on his left. Mountain peaks cut jagged spires against the sky behind him, the shimmering sun backlighting them and forcing him to squint.

The gray acted nervous and skittish, even after the rabbit was long gone. Again Touch the Sky glanced behind him, blinded in the fierce light.

Scattered clumps of cottonwood trees could easily hide pursuers.

A premonition of danger moved up his spine like the ticklish touch of a feather.

He placed a hand on the gray's thick white mane and spoke gently to her. It was almost time to make camp for the night. He veered closer to the river, planning to find a good patch of graze in which to tether his pony.

Suddenly, a sharp tug just below his ribs was followed immediately by a white-hot pain in his left side that made him cry out.

Touch the Sky looked down and recognized a Pawnee arrowhead protruding from his body, the honed tip shiny with his blood!

Then his hackles rose when, with a thundering of hooves, his unseen enemies raised a triumphant war cry and charged him.

Chapter Four

Touch the Sky knew the Pawnee were excellent horsemen. He was as good as dead if he attempted to outrun them across the wide-open prairie and sage flats.

Instead, he veered hard to the north, toward the Bighorn Mountains and the Yellowstone with its protective thickets.

His side felt like it was on fire. But hearing the bloodthirsty whoops and yips behind him made him forget the pain. The gray surged forward, laying her ears back flat as Touch the Sky prodded her flanks with his heels.

She was well rested from the slow pace earlier. Now, as the stolen Crow pony opened up the distance between Touch the Sky and his pursuers, he realized what a magnificent animal she was.

By the time the sun dropped below the horizon, the Pawnee were no longer in sight behind him.

Touch the Sky slowed his mount from a gallop to a run to a canter. Despite the fall of darkness and the fiery pain lancing through his wounded side, he knew he was dead if he stopped. The Pawnee were in their element after dark. He knew they could read the star-shot heavens as easily as a Cheyenne read sign along a game trail.

He ate some dried plums from his legging sash. But increasingly, he became aware of an overpowering thirst. Distracted with worry when he had ridden out of camp, he had foolishly neglected to fill a bladder-bag with water. Nor, after this hard run, could the gray go much longer without drinking.

He knew this new course was unlikely to cross any water before he reached the Yellowstone. But he couldn't afford to waste time searching for it.

He slowed the gray to a long trot and held that pace. Constantly, he turned one ear to listen behind him. At one point, when the gray faltered slightly topping a rise, he halted her for a brief rest.

Wincing at the pain which flared up in his side, he slid to the ground and dropped down on all fours. Placing one ear to the ground, he listened long and carefully. He heard or felt nothing, and relaxed slightly until the next burst of pain jolted him back to the reality of his danger.

He knew he would have to deal with the arrow before the wound swelled closed around it. But he also knew that removing the arrow would increase the bleeding. And on the open plains, there was plenty of time to bleed to death.

He could tell, by the location of the Grandmother Star to the north, that the night was well advanced. Mounting again was even more painful than dismounting. Speaking gently to the gray, he stroked her neck. Then he nudged her flanks.

Reluctantly, expecting a long, cool drink of water as reward for her hard work, the tough little pony snorted in protest before she obeyed.

"He is bleeding, but not heavily. The blood has not yet stiffened. He cannot be far from here."

Gun Powder knelt atop a long rise where the Cheyenne had obviously stopped, judging from the prints, both hoof and moccasin. The blood was clearly visible in the unclouded light of a full moon.

Red Plume stared at a brave named Iron Knife, anger tightening his face.

"You squirrel-brained fool! How could you have missed the pony and hit the Cheyenne? For this you will forfeit a coup feather. He is no good to us if he bleeds to death!"

Iron Knife said nothing. He stared straight ahead and showed nothing in his face. He was ashamed of his failure with his bow. But he had no respect for Red Plume or his clan, not one of whom dared face his knife. There was much talk of taking his coup feathers away. Yet no one in the tribe had ever gotten close enough to pluck them out of his bonnet.

"It is a fast pony," said Gun Powder. "A strong pony. But without water it will weaken. We can catch him this night if we ride hard."

Red Plume nodded. Idly, as he considered the best course of action, he picked a louse from the grease in his top-knot and cracked it between strong white teeth.

"Then we ride hard!" he said. "Before the morning star is born, he will lie under our lances!"

Twice during the long night Touch the Sky heard the distant sounds of his enemy behind him. Reluctantly, his wounded side throbbing at the increased jolting, he pushed the thirsty and tired gray to a long gallop.

Thus he opened the distance between himself and his pursuers. But by now his thirst was so powerful it overshadowed the pain of his wound. He sucked on pebbles to keep moisture in his mouth.

Finally, as his sister the sun began to color the eastern horizon pink, he was unable to bear his thirst any longer.

There was nothing he could do yet for his pony. But Touch the Sky veered right from his course when he spotted a rocky spine rising out of the plains. It had rained recently. He recalled a trick that old Knobby, a former mountain man who was now the hostler back in Bighorn Falls, had told him about.

Slowed considerably by his stiffening wound, he dismounted, hobbled his pony, and picked his way up toward the boulders at the very top of the spine. As he had hoped, the hollows of the larger rocks still held precious drops of rainwater. Gratefully, he moved from boulder to boulder, lowering his lips to the night-cooled water and lapping it up like an animal.

It was only a few swallows, all tolled. But the water blunted the harshest edge of his thirst. Before he climbed back down to his pony, he scanned the plains to the south.

His mouth tightened into a grim slit when he saw riders profiled against the new day's horizon. They were the size of insects at this distance. But a slight lead on a thirsty and nearly exhausted pony meant nothing on the plains.

His wound throbbed with insistent pain as he climbed back down to his mount. Now that the sun was rising, he decided to veer northeast—riding into the new sun would make him a more difficult target next time the Pawnee attacked.

Speaking softly to his pony, explaining that there was no other choice, he mounted and reluctantly pushed northward.

"The Cheyenne buck stopped here to drink."

Gun Powder's voice was raised so it would carry down to the others. They sat their ponies at the base of the rocky spine, watching the keen-eyed warrior read the boulders for sign.

"He has ridden into the sun," said the Pawnee brave called Iron Knife. He squatted on the ground, examining the prints leading away from the spine.

"Our enemy has tough battle bark on him. He has decided we must *earn* the right to dangle his scalp from our coup stick," said their leader, Red Plume.

The warrior's tone showed approval of their quarry's survival spirit. The Cheyenne had raised their battle axes forever against the Pawnee. This one knew full well what fate awaited him if— *when*—Red Plume's Pawnee braves seized him.

There was no question that he would soon watch crows and vultures pick at his guts, pulled out of his body coil by coil before his own eyes. Pawnee scouting ability was respected even by the Bluecoats themselves. The red "men of men" were considered the U.S. Army's most capable mercenaries—they formed the backbone of special Indian-hunting units which had razed more than one Cheyenne, Sioux, Arapahoe, and Shoshone village.

Those who called this "treachery" had forgotten the ancient wrongs against the Pawnee. The Sioux and the Cheyenne had joined forces to drive them south from the Powder River country, hoarding the vast buffalo herds for themselves. Pawnee children died of starvation while, to the north, buffalo meat lay rotting.

Soon, thought Red Plume, the just anger of the supernatural father, Tirawa, would demand another bloody retribution from the Cheyenne. Not just this lone warrior or the annual ritual of sacrificing a captured maiden—often a Cheyenne—to the Morning Star. This time the entire Cheyenne nation must atone with blood.

"He is a warrior," said Red Plume. "A sly one. However, *nothing* lies between us and the river but empty plains. A frog is slippery—in the water. But it is easily crushed on dry land."

He glanced up at the spine again and gestured impatiently to Gun Powder. "Hurry! Now we ride hard and crush our frog!"

The sun was well up and casting short shadows. Dull pain throbbed like a tight tourniquet in Touch the Sky's wounded side. By now thirst had caked his mouth like parched alkali soil, a raw, dry grittiness that filled his throat and left his belly cramping.

The gray too was weak with water starvation. Even at a slow trot she faltered often. Now he had to fight her more and more to keep her pointed northeast—some instinct made her want to try another direction.

Finally, tired of fighting her, Touch the Sky gave her her head and let the gray set her own pace and direction. She veered sharply to the west, breaking from a trot into a lope which soon became a run.

Abruptly, she drew up short in a slight, wide, dry depression that formed a winding path across the vast prairie.

Puzzled, even through the increasing fog of his exhaustion, pain, and delirium, Touch the Sky stroked the pure white mane.

"This is a dry streambed," he told his pony. "The water is long gone. You smell a memory, just a memory."

But the gray nickered impatiently, turned her head, pawed the ground hard.

His jaw set firmly against the pain, Touch the Sky dismounted and sank to his knees, staring hard at the depressions where the gray had dug up the dirt.

It looked darker than dry earth should—and felt slightly damp to his touch.

He gouged his fingers into the deepest print and probed even deeper.

When his fingers came back out, there was mud under the nails!

Unsheathing his knife, ignoring the pain in his side now, Touch the Sky dug frantically. A few minutes of digging exposed a thin layer of seepage.

He dug deeper, and soon a little pool had formed.

Giving thanks to Maiyun and the four directions, Touch the Sky dropped his face into the pool. Forcing himself to take measured swallows, he drank his fill. Then he widened the hole and rose to let the gray follow suit.

His legs were still weak with hunger. Touch the

Sky ate some pemmican and dried fruit from his legging sash while the gray drank and rested. Now, he told himself, they must ride hard toward the valley of the Yellowstone. His wound had swollen dangerously tight around the arrow. It had to be removed, and he had to sleep.

The pony had grazed lush grass all spring. Now, refreshed by the water, she resumed her hard pace.

Touch the Sky rode until his shadow was lengthening in the westering sun. Finally, topping a long rise, he spotted the first coarse-barked cottonwood trees with their leathery leaves. He had finally reached the winding valley of the Yellowstone.

His enemies were still trailing him—the last time he had listened to the ground, he had felt them approaching at a rapid pace. Now he led the gray into the river and followed the current downstream until he was sure he had made it difficult for the Pawnee to pick up his trail again.

He rode up out of the water and into a protective line of thickets. This was Crow country. So first he checked the ground all around him. He read the old and fresh tracks of weasel, mink, wolf, and cougar and knew it was safe—animals would not be so abundant in an area where humans were.

Touch the Sky found a nearby clearing amidst the thicket. He hobbled his pony in the patch of browse. Then he set to work building a crude brush lean-to in which to hide. He covered it over with branches and brambles, until it looked like a natural deadfall.

He threw his buffalo robe inside. By now the sun was sending her last feeble rays up against the encroaching night sky. Touch the Sky was now prepared for that which he had been dreading.

First he found a stand of spruce trees and dug some balsam sap from one. From a red willow he peeled strips of soft bark. Then he returned to his brush lean-to and crawled inside.

Wincing, he snapped the fletching off of the Pawnee arrow. Then, setting his jaw, he jerked the arrow out forward in one sharp tug.

White hot fire licked at his side, and a field of black dots danced in front of his eyes. Hurrying to get it done before he passed out, he packed the ragged, angry edges of his wound with balsam. Then he bound it with strips of the bark.

His ministrations left him exhausted. He collapsed back into his robe. Within moments he was sleeping like a dead man, even as the nearby Pawnee searched desperately for his trail.

Chapter Five

He woke to clear morning light and the scolding of jays, angry at this human intrusion into their nesting grounds.

But the warbling song of the nearby purple finch told Touch the Sky no one else was lurking in the area. Cautiously, he rose to a sitting position in the lean-to. Pain jolted through his wounded side. He eased outside for a better look.

A cold apprehension iced his stomach when he saw the ragged, discolored edges of his wound. The balsam had eased the burning pain. But he had waited too long to remove the arrow— now the wound was contaminated deep inside. A greenish-yellow discharge oozed from the torn flesh.

He checked on his pony and led her down to the river to drink. Then he moved her to a new patch of browse, still hidden within the thickets.

By midday he was light-headed. He realized he needed fresh meat for strength and to fight the infection. This close to the river, small game was plentiful. He killed a rabbit, gutted and skinned it, then used the same arrow he'd shot it with as a spit, running it lengthwise through the rabbit.

He built a small fire while the sun was highest, which made the smoke and flames hard to see. As soon as the meat was charred enough to eat, he put the fire out. He also followed the precaution, after he'd devoured the rabbit, of moving further upriver in case the smoke had been spotted.

Well past midday, a new brush lean-to constructed, Touch the Sky began to relax. By now it appeared that he had successfully thrown the Pawnee off his scent. They must, he decided, be well out of this area. But when he ventured closer to the water's edge, he discovered he was wrong.

He first spotted the tracks in a patch of lush marsh marigold. Many tracks, leading up and down the river bank several times. They were made by unshod Indian ponies, and judging from the sharp bend of the crushed marigolds, the latest set were made quite recently.

Meaning the Pawnee probably remained in the area, searching for him.

Knowing the lice-eaters' skill at tracking, Touch the Sky realized it was only a matter of time before they closed in on him.

He considered his plight. The infection in his wound would soon severely limit his ability to travel very far across wide-open plains. The Pawnee would simply trail him like wolves stalking a wounded buffalo, merely waiting for him to drop. Nor could he stay here in the river valley—even if he could stay hidden, his pony would eventually be discovered.

No, thought Touch the Sky—neither plains nor river valley would do. He glanced south, toward the snowcapped peaks of the Bighorn Mountains.

His best chance for survival now was to take to the high country.

The Ute tribe lived high up in those peaks. They had been driven there by Sioux and Cheyenne after it was learned they were cooperating with Bluecoat pony soldiers. However, the turncoat Pawnee were also currently at war with the Ute.

Touch the Sky knew it would be easier for him to flee alone unnoticed into the mountains than it would be for the Pawnee band. They were not likely to ride far up into the hostile high country merely to capture one enemy.

The country between the river valley and the mountains was mostly flat, sparsely forested tableland and plains. Despite the Pawnee skill with star charts, he knew his only chance lay in leaving after darkness fell.

Again he checked on the gray, leading her to water before he tethered her in a sheltered patch of graze. Then he tended to his wound. He cleaned it as best he could and repacked it with balsam. Afterward, he rested inside the lean-to, preparing for his journey.

Nightfall brought clouds and light rain, which quickly gave way to a starlit sky and a full moon. Touch the Sky went down to the river to drink and cleanse his wound one more time. By now his side had swollen even more, the jagged mouth of the wound oozing pus. He was light-headed, feverish, and his weak legs felt hamstrung.

The fat moon and all the stars worried him. Before he retrieved his pony he rubbed his body down with mud to cut reflection. Then he squatted and concentrated on the most important survival skill his warrior training had taught him: freeing his mind of useless thoughts and paying attention instead to the language of nature.

All seemed well. The sparrow hawks which thickened the treetops near the water remained undisturbed. Frogs sent out their eerie, croaking rhythm, the hum of cicadas and crickets was unbroken. Prowling owls hooted to each other across the shadowy expanse of the murmuring river.

Now the time was right. If Pawnee were lurking nearby, they had cleverly fooled even nature herself.

But as he rose and started back toward the lean-to, his wounded side protested with a painful throbbing. Once he was forced to stop and sink to his knees until strength returned to his legs.

Again he glanced toward the peaks of the Bighorns, dark shapes against the blue-black night sky. Would he even be able to make the ride in this condition? But he had no choice. It was either ride for his life, or surrender it here.

He dropped one hand to his medicine pouch and offered a brief prayer to Maiyun. Then he went to retrieve his weapons and his pony.

*   *   *

"He knew it was foolish to stay hidden here. His wound bothers him greatly, but he has wisely run to the mountains. The tracks are fresh, but so is his pony. It has drunk and grazed and rested."

Gun Powder rose from the set of prints leading away from the river thickets toward the outlying plains and the distant Bighorn Mountains.

"He avoided us well," said Red Plume, still sitting his horse. "We passed this spot many times, searching. Our Cheyenne buck knows how to play the fox."

"His pony," said Gun Powder, "was captured from the Crow."

He pointed to the prints. In the bright wash of a full moon, looking closely, he could see the slight cleft made by the back of the hoof—the distinctive print of the stocky mountain breed preferred by the Crow tribe, allies in battle of the Pawnee.

"If he counted coup on a Crow brave," said Red Plume, "he is a warrior of the first rank."

"Then, why not let him go?" asked one of the other four braves riding with Red Plume and Gun Powder. "We can capture another Cheyenne. Why ride into the teeth of our enemies, the Ute?"

"I too am not eager to face Ute in their stronghold," said Red Plume. "But only think on this thing. This buck we track knows by now that we are Pawnee. We cannot be sure that Yellow Bear's tribe knows yet that we are in the Powder River country. If we let him go, and he returns to his clan circle, the entire Cheyenne nation will soon know that we have slipped into their hunting grounds.

"No, brothers! Iron Knife failed his tribe when

he aimed wrong. Now there is nothing else for it but to finish the work Iron Knife's arrow has begun. And with luck, we will also learn the secret of exactly when and where the Cheyenne will be holding their chief-renewal ceremony."

Red Plume looked at Gun Powder again. "You say his pony is fresh. But as you also say, his wound troubles him greatly. Quickly, mount up! With this moon turning night into day, we can ride hard and catch him before he even reaches the mountains."

He rode hard across the open country, his mind playing cat and mouse with consciousness. At one moment the infection in his wound made him feel feverish; a moment later chills would sweep through him, turning the clammy sweat cold all over him.

Only the occasional stand of scrub pine and cedar broke the monotonous, vast emptiness around him. In the moonlight he felt vulnerable, constantly observed. He slowed to rest the gray. Almost immediately, a bitch wolf began slinking along behind him, tenacious but keeping her distance.

Then Touch the Sky realized: He was giving off the stink of death! Wolves never attacked humans—they merely trailed them when they sensed death was near at hand, patiently waiting for nature to provide a meal.

At one point, when he was perhaps halfway to the foothills, he stopped his pony at the top of a long rise. By now his side was hot and throbbing, sending fiery tentacles of pain throughout his body when he dismounted. Lining himself up with the huge yellow moon, he stared out across the wavering plains for a long time until he was sure he detected the movement of riders following him. They were outlined against the huge saffron moon behind them—vague, shimmering shapes that drew gradually closer.

The lice-eaters had picked up his trail! Touch the Sky spoke to his pony; then, face crumpling at the pain, he mounted and dug his heels hard into her flanks.

"Hi-ya!" He shouted the battle cry to rally both of them.

Later, he would have no memory of that grueling race across the flats with death literally at his heels. He drove the gray mercilessly until she faltered, then slowed to a long trot to rest her. He continued this pattern, never once stopping. At one point, he started awake and realized he had been unconscious— how long, he didn't know. But if he fell from the saddle now, in his condition, his scalp was as good as dangling from a Pawnee coup stick.

While he was still lucid enough to do so, he freed one of the buffalo-hair ropes he used as a long tether for the pony. Wrapping it around his waist, carefully avoiding the aching wound, he then ran it through the pony's hackamore and under her belly like a surcingle, a strap used as a handhold when riding a mean horse. He then tied it around his waist again, securing himself.

He rode as if through a thick but patchy fog. For moments his eyes would snap open and he could see the distant peaks of the mountains, looming closer each time. Then the undertow of delirium would suck him under again, and for long spells he was unconscious while the gray set her own pace.

Once, toward sunrise, he turned again to search the flats behind him. He didn't need the aid of the moon now.

The Pawnee had steadily closed the distance. He spotted them, skylined on top of a ridge against the lightening sky. He could count the shapes now—six of them.

Fear keeping him awake, he finally gained the foothills as the sun burst forth over the horizon. Soon he was following a winding trail which snaked its way steadily higher through meadows of beautiful columbine and bright mountain laurel.

Every time he glanced back, pain stabbing through his side, he could see the Pawnee even nearer. The morning sun glistened on their shaved skulls and greased topknots, highlighted the brilliant streamers flying from their lances. They had been riding six abreast, but now rode single file along the narrow mountain trail.

Somewhere above, thought Touch the Sky, lurked Ute eager to raise the hair of Cheyenne or Pawnee. How far would the lice-eaters pursue him?

Despite the lost ground, he decided to stop briefly so he and the gray could drink from a streamlet. He dipped his head under the surface of the ice-cold water, the shock momentarily sharpening his senses again. He unwrapped his

side and tried not to give in to fear when he saw
how red and savage and swollen the wound had
become. A putrid stink like carrion assaulted his
nostrils.

He immersed in the cold water, the pain
momentarily abating. But already he could hear
the distant shouts of his Pawnee pursuers,
pumping blood into their eyes by singing their
battle songs.

The rest did the sturdy mountain pony good.
Soon she had gained back some of the lost ground
as her superior breeding began to pay off in
the higher altitudes. She was able to scamper
effortlessly where Touch the Sky thought only
sure-footed mules could go.

As they were about to break out above the
tree line, the gray suddenly shied and nervously
side-jumped. Fearing ambush by Ute, Touch the
Sky instead spotted a black bear well back from
the trail. It ignored him, rolling a log over to
look for insects. He calmed his pony and quickly
urged her higher—all horses instinctively hated
and feared bears, and some had been known to
panic, killing their riders in headlong rushes
over cliffs.

He began to fade in and out of awareness again
as they pushed even higher, past wind-wrung
trees stubbornly growing from cracks in rocks.
The faint trail gave way to rock-strewn, dangerous slopes which sometimes rose precipitously.
Twice the powerful gray slipped and lost her
footing. Jolted hard, Touch the Sky was forced
to cry out at the explosion of fiery hurt in his
side.

Despite his determination, he passed out for

some time. He woke only when the gray suddenly halted, refusing to climb further.

Then he saw why: a huge rock slide had wiped out much of the slope above, the mass of the boulders and rocks forming a huge choke-point in front of him when they reached a narrow defile. Though the narrow opening had stopped most of them, they had jumbled into and over it with overwhelming weight. Now the slide was balanced on the feather edge, ready to hurtle on downward at the slightest nudge.

A nudge as slight as the weight of one pony.

Touch the Sky carefully skirted the dangerous area, riding well to the left of the loose scree. But now he was so weak that only the rope rigging held him on horseback. There was no other choice: He would have to risk a hiding place long enough to rest.

Above the rock slide, a lone boulder had been stopped by a granite outcropping. Touch the Sky made for its apron of shade. He scarcely mustered enough energy to dismount and hobble his pony in the shade of the outcropping before exhaustion turned his limbs to water. He crawled behind the boulder.

He dropped into a fitful, troubling sleep, his breath rasping in his throat. Reality fused with dreams. He heard the Pawnee war cry, heard the harsh, sharp, precise twang of their osage bows. He heard women and children crying, dying horses nickering, smelled the sheared-metal tang of blood—rivers of blood.

Most disturbing of all was the unsettling image which plagued Touch the Sky during his delirium sleep: the image of a huge snake, a snake larger than any he had ever seen, its perfectly hinged jaws open wide as it swallowed a full-grown horse!

But then one of the dream noises became more real than the others, somehow seemed closer.

When his eyes snapped open, the sun blazed straight into them. At the same moment, no more than a good stone's throw down the slope, the triumphant Pawnee raised their voices in shrill war cries as they spotted his pony.

Chapter Six

Pushing their ponies hard, avoiding paleface wagon tracks, Wolf Who Hunts Smiling and Swift Canoe rode due east toward the Black Hills and sacred Medicine Lake.

They already knew this was Touch the Sky's destination. Arrow Keeper had made the announcement about Touch the Sky's supposedly important mission for the tribe. But Black Elk, their war leader, had given *them* an important mission too.

Only theirs was a mission of death.

Had they taken time to read the signs, they would quickly have learned that their quarry was being pursued in a different direction. But they couldn't waste valuable time—he had one sleep's lead on them. Their plan was to ride fast like hawks swept along in a fierce wind and arrive at Medicine Lake before him. Black Elk, however, had announced to the tribe that they were only riding south to the Platte River to scout for Pawnee.

Shortly after they were out of sight of the curious eyes of the sentries, Wolf Who Hunts Smiling said, "I know a shorter way."

He veered away from the familiar game trail and pointed his pure black pony northeast. The country here was more wooded and far less dangerous to ride because there were few prairie dog holes to trip a horse. However, it was occasionally patrolled by Bluecoat logging details from the soldiertown just south of the Little Missouri River.

"Brother," said Swift Canoe when they stopped to water their ponies at a buffalo wallow. "A thing troubles me."

"Then speak of it," said Wolf Who Hunts Smiling. His furtive, swift eyes constantly scanned the surrounding ridges and cut to their backtrail.

Swift Canoe could not quite admit that he had attempted to kill Touch the Sky but failed. It happened when Swift Canoe and River of Winds had been sent to Bighorn Falls to spy on Touch the Sky and Little Horse. Now he only said:

"Like yours, my heart is nothing but stone toward Woman Face. He killed my brother! I agree with Black Elk. He must be killed for the good of the tribe. But this one thing troubles me, this drawing of Cheyenne blood so near our sacred lake. Can we not kill him sooner and avoid defiling the Arrows?"

Wolf Who Hunts Smiling had thought of this too. As usual he said nothing when Swift Canoe accused Touch the Sky of killing his brother, True Son. Wolf Who Hunts Smiling, of all members of the tribe, knew full well that Touch the Sky had not caused True Son's death. But he also remembered seeing his own father turned into stew meat by Bluecoat canister shot. He hated all whites, and this "Cheyenne" intruder was one of their dogs!

Still—the act of murdering another Cheyenne, even a stinking turncoat, was so heinous that the same Cheyenne word for "putrid" was applied to murderers. This was because murder began a man's internal corruption. About the murderer there clung the rotten smell. Murder brought the tribe bad luck. There could be no success in war; there could be no bounty in the hunt because game shunned the territory. Murderers were not allowed to eat or smoke from Cheyenne utensils for fear of polluting them.

Wolf Who Hunts Smiling did not believe all the nonsense repeated by the tribal elders. But this belief about murderers was strong.

"Have you never thought," he said, "that the hand of Maiyun is in this thing? Have you never thought that it is *He* who has selected the place where this enemy is to go under?"

Swift Canoe remained silent, considering this. Wolf Who Hunts Smiling was a fiery, convincing speaker.

"Have you never thought," he added, "that the Supernatural is angry at this 'Cheyenne' who speaks more than one way? This 'Cheyenne' who does not believe yet has been sent to have a vision—mocking our God and our faith?"

Swift Canoe nodded. His nostrils flared as his

breathing increased to match his anger.

"You speak the straight word, brother!"

"Only think on this thing," said Wolf Who Hunts Smiling. "Has this stranger not placed strong medicine over the eyes of our elders? He rides into our camp, stinking of the white man's ways. But do the elders protect their tribe from this danger?"

Swift Canoe shook his head, dark eyes snapping sparks of bitter resentment. "They do not, brother! Led by Arrow Keeper's example they blind their eyes to his faults and show him special consideration."

"I have ears for this! Have *we*, who never once hid in our clan lodge while the war cry sounded, ever been honored by a tribal council as he has?"

"Never," said Swift Canoe. "They are too busy fawning over their pet to notice our bravery."

"Nor do we turn our war leader into a gelding by holding his squaw in our blanket. This white man's dog would rut on our Cheyenne women! Hear this, buck! This is not the killing of a fellow Cheyenne. We are killing a dangerous enemy for the good of the tribe.

"Now mount, warrior! The only 'vision' this dog will see is the sight of my lance spilling his guts."

Touch the Sky's bow and foxskin quiver lay beside him. He slipped the notch of a fire-hardened arrow onto his bowstring and drew it taut. Then he peered cautiously around the shelter of the precariously balanced boulder.

The Pawnee were taking up positions down the slope from him, below the narrow, rock-clogged defile. Clearly, they were not sure yet exactly where he was hiding.

Touch the Sky realized the gray was in a vulnerable spot. He laid his bow down. Without revealing his position, he reached out beyond the boulder and undid her rawhide hobble. Then he picked up a light, round stone and tossed it at her, bouncing it off her flank. Unhurt but startled, the pony fled back over the shoulder of the mountain, out of range.

Soon the Pawnee sent a scout up on the right flank, skirting the rock slide to get a good side view of the defile. They suspected, thought Touch the Sky, that he had taken cover somewhere in the defile.

It was important to keep them thinking that way.

Wincing at the powerful pain, he rose to his elbows and then his knees, bow in his hands. Again he drew the string taut as he sighted on the crawling brave.

The Pawnee rose for a moment, craning to peer around a scraggly bush. The next instant Touch the Sky's arrow pierced his left cheek, skewered his tongue, broke several teeth, and punched out through his right cheek.

Though the arrow effectively trapped his mouth shut, the Pawnee raised a hideous shriek of pain. He scuttled back down toward his waiting companions. Blood streamed from both sides of his face.

Touch the Sky was in too much pain himself to feel any elation. His shot had bought him some time—but what good was time if he passed out again?

This time, still thinking he was holed up in the defile, the Pawnee tried sending a point man up the scree-covered left flank.

This was an awkward angle for Touch the Sky, since he had to either face exposure or use his left arm to pull the bowstring.

His arrow missed the sentry by a hand's-breadth. But it sent the lice-eater scuttling back down the slope on all fours like a panicked bug.

Now the Pawnee hunkered down out of sight. For a long time Touch the Sky fought to keep his eyes open, tossed from one wave to another on a turbulent sea of pain.

The sun climbed even higher overhead, its rays finally starting to warm up the night-cooled boulder.

Still, the Pawnee waited.

His eyes trembled, then closed. His head slacked forward until his chin bumped his chest.

He started awake, fear like a metallic dust coating his tongue. But still no movement from below the defile.

The sun beat down on him mercilessly. Absently, he popped a few pebbles in his mouth and sucked on them to slake his thirst.

The sun inched toward her resting place, and still the Pawnee did not move. Again and again Touch the Sky caught himself fading out.

Finally, as the shadow of the boulder was lengthening in the late sun, Touch the Sky began to suspect the lice-eaters had tricked him. Perhaps they had left long ago.

Or perhaps they were even now preparing to rush over the shoulder of the mountain behind him.

A sudden prickle of apprehension made him turn to look up the slope behind him. The Pawnee chose that moment to charge, shrieking madly, from their hidden positions below him.

There were five of them now. This time they avoided the flanks, scrambling straight up over the tumble of scree. Despite the danger of provoking another slide, they leaped nimbly from boulder to boulder. And now, as arrows whipped past his ears with a humming sound like bumblebees, he realized they had figured out his position.

He notched an arrow, launched it, notched another, and sent it flying. But he had little time to aim past shields, and his enemies danced like the mating Hako birds of their elaborate spring ceremony, throwing his aim off.

The first Pawnee, blood lust gleaming in his eyes, scrambled into the rock-strewn defile. Touch the Sky considered running in the direction he had sent his horse. But he knew he would never outrun them in his weakened condition.

"Yip-yip-yiii!" screamed the lead Pawnee. He raised a double-bladed throwing ax over his head to rally his comrades.

Another arrow glanced off the boulder. Reflexively, Touch the Sky drew back. As he did so, he lost his balance and fell against the delicately positioned boulder.

It moved slightly. Only one edge of the granite outcropping kept it from hurtling downward.

Downward!

"Yip-yip-yiii!" Closer. The Pawnee was halfway across the huge jumble of fallen boulders, his companions close on the heels of his quilled moccasins.

Willing strength into his exhausted body, Touch the Sky leaned one shoulder into the boulder and heaved.

Nothing. He shoved again, hard, until his wounded side flared in a protest of pain. This time the boulder moved a little, a rivulet of dirt sliding down the slope.

"Yip-yip-yiii!"

The lead Pawnee was so close that Touch the Sky could make out the beadwork on his medicine bundle.

Again he leaned hard into the boulder, the pain in his wound so great now that he almost blacked out.

Suddenly the outcropping crumpled, and a moment later the boulder was tumbling down the slope.

The lead Pawnee barely leaped aside in time as the huge boulder, a hurtling juggernaut now, slammed into the loose, huge pile of scree. For a moment all was silent, time suspended as the huge slide seemed to shudder like a beast waking up.

The next moment, the earth seemed to cave in on herself. There was a huge, grinding roar; a cloud of dust puffed up and blocked the sun; the mountainside became a living, heaving thing.

A startled shouting rose from the frightened Pawnee. Behind them, their panicked horses rolled their eyes until they were all milky whites, straining to break their tethers.

The last thing Touch the Sky saw was a Pawnee disappearing in a cloud of sliding dirt and rock. The Cheyenne gave quick thanks to the four directions of the wind. But he didn't remain behind to see the results of his man-made disaster.

His face melting into a mask of pain with each step, he ran up the slope behind him. Now his life depended on how far the gray had wandered.

Chapter Seven

"Scalp Cane was sent under," said the Pawnee brave named Iron Knife. "Roan Bear's legs have been broken. We will need to lash together a travois for both of them. I have removed the arrow from Short Buffalo's face. But he will be unable to ride for several sleeps."

Red Plume nodded. His face was drawn tight in profile as he turned to stare in the direction the Cheyenne had fled. Red Plume had led the charge and barely leaped aside in time to avoid being crushed in the slide. A huge, grape-colored bruise covered the side of his face where he had landed hard when he jumped.

"He has cut our number in half. And killed my best pony," he said bitterly. "The best battle pony I have ever trained. Now it is maggot fodder under those boulders. I must ride Scalp Cane's pony."

Both warriors knew well what he meant: Riding

the pony of a dead warrior was considered bad luck. Red Plume no longer took joy in this hunt. He had even lost interest in the prospect of wringing information from their most hated enemy, the Cheyenne. He only wanted to capture this red dog—to have the pleasure of staking him out spread-eagle in the blazing sun after slicing his eyelids off.

"Find his trail," he told Gun Powder. "I swear this on my medicine bundle. For the Pawnee blood he has spilled, we will smear his blood on our faces!"

Even as Red Plume swore his oath, Touch the Sky was backtracking past the Pawnee at dangerously close range.

At first, after he started the slide, luck had been with the wounded, feverish Cheyenne: The well-trained gray had waited patiently just past the shoulder of the mountain.

But soon his luck ran out. The mountainside down which the sure-footed pony climbed had abruptly sheared off in a steep cliff. Unbroken rock wall plunged straight down to a jumbled mass of talus, rock fragments, far below.

He rode desperately to either side, but the cliff wrapped around this entire half of the mountain. There was no choice but to double back, dangerously close to the rock slide and the Pawnee.

He knew some had survived. Touch the Sky had heard them shouting to each other after the first thunderous din had abated.

Before he rode back over the shoulder, he dug four small but thick pieces of elk hide out of the chamois pannier tied to his horse. Rallying himself against the pain, he slid off the gray. It was a slow, painful process, but he tied all four pieces to the gray's hooves with rawhide thongs.

Touch the Sky had first learned the trick from Arrow Keeper. Even though most Indians did not shoe their ponies, in the high country there was plenty of stone and flint. It could ring loudly when struck by a horse's hoof.

He stole back down the mountain, leading his pony through an erosion gully that came within a stone's throw of the Pawnee survivors. Luckily, they were busy tending to the injured. No doubt they assumed he was long gone.

He realized now that he could not possibly stay in the high country. The Pawnee had braved a Ute attack to follow him. They would never give up their search now that he had their blood on his hands. His best hope lay in getting as much head start as possible before his wound forced him to hole up.

His journey back down out of the mountains in the gathering darkness was tense but uneventful. Once he passed a spot where the Ute had set up racks to smoke fish. Every moment he expected to hear either the deep-chested kill cry of the Ute or the shrill and unnerving Pawnee shriek. But he finally reached the foothills and then the moonlit plain without being challenged.

His infected side was approaching its crisis stage. Again he drifted back and forth between waking and sleeping. Again he was forced to lash himself to his pony to keep from dropping off her.

At first the gray had been pointed east toward the Black Hills. But as Touch the Sky drifted into his feverish fancies, the pony was spooked by a coyote. She began to follow her own course toward the vast, empty northern country.

Touch the Sky rode, unaware of his direction or surroundings, until the weary gray faltered and simply refused to go further. By now, the sun long gone, fever chills wracked the Cheyenne's exhausted body.

He slid off his pony and nearly fell, his legs were so weak. Touch the Sky was too exhausted to hobble his pony. He found a huge boulder that still retained the heat of the day. He sprawled against it, hugging the hard, warm surface.

Again that night, as he passed in and out of the fog of delirium, he experienced the strange medicine vision of earlier: a vision of a huge, winding snake swallowing a horse.

He awoke in the desolate time just after dawn, when all the colors of the plains still form a gray, unbroken mass. His wound was festering. It leaked a greenish-yellow discharge that stank sweetly of rot and death. But the deep, exhausted sleep had rested him.

Stiff and sore, he climbed down from the boulder. His pony grazed a patch of nearby grass. She nickered in greeting.

Touch the Sky stared back toward the mountains, watching close for movement on the horizon. But he saw no sign yet of the Pawnee.

He was badly disoriented and realized he had drifted far off course. This far north the country was unfamiliar. He could not recognize the landmarks which would lead him to Medicine Lake.

His hopes sinking even further, he took in the vast, strange landscape. When his name was still Matthew Hanchon he had read Zebulon Pike's famous charge: The land west of the Mississippi River was "the Great American Desert," arid and empty and useless. The mountain men's explorations had proved Pike wrong—though vast, it was a land of riches. And the red man was in the way of those riches, according to the whites.

Still, Touch the Sky understood why the whites back East called this a desert—this was territory so desolate and huge that a rider without a remount was a dead man if his horse foundered.

But Touch the Sky had to cross it, to find his way to Medicine Lake. He had to elude the Pawnee in search, Arrow Keeper insisted, of a vision.

He knew that the vision Arrow Keeper meant was not the brief, horse-devouring-snake image of his dream. It would be a vast and epic vision, the old shaman insisted.

But even if he sought and obtained a vision, thought Touch the Sky, it could still be bad medicine. Arrow Keeper had explained this to him when Touch the Sky sought a vision before attacking the white whiskey traders. Now the old medicine man's words crept into his thoughts like a whispered warning:

A medicine vision can be either a revelation or a curse. An enemy's strong medicine may place a false vision over our eyes, and we may act upon it, aiding our enemies and destroying those whom we seek to help.

Even as he thought these things, his wound throbbed ominously. He whistled and the gray trotted obediently over to him.

Getting on his pony was a major effort which left tears of pain in his eyes. He wanted to rest for a few more hours.

But fear prodded him as he recalled the fate of those who had provoked Pawnee vengeance.

Vision Quest

* * *

Touch the Sky rode until his shadow was long and distorted in the dying sun. Though he headed east, he had no idea how far south he needed to go nor when he needed to turn.

His supply of pemmican and dried fruit was gone. At one point, skirting a long spine of hills, he spotted a whitetail deer. He shot but missed, losing another arrow because he could not risk the time searching for it. He was dangerously low now, his quiver almost empty.

But he had a more immediate problem than even hunger: his wound. Now he was constantly feverish as his body tried to fight off the infection. By sunset he felt like one huge, exposed wound.

Now, with the instincts of a sick animal, he only wanted to hole up until the crisis was over. At this point either prospect—survival or death—was the same to him.

He stopped at a runoff stream which cut through a copse of trees. Touch the Sky turned the gray loose to drink. He was unable now to bend down so he could tether her. That night the exhausted, delirious Cheyenne crawled into a dense stand of spruce. Then he passed out on a deep mat of needles.

He didn't wake up until the sun had almost completed her morning journey. He was clear-headed, famished, and realized he had survived his crisis.

The wound was still stiff and sore. But the discharge was almost gone, and the swelling was down. Touch the Sky carefully cleaned it and wrapped his side with soft bark to protect it.

Now he faced that other life-threatening crisis, the worm that gnawed slower but just as sure: starvation.

Game on the plains was scarce this far north. As for buffalo, the herds had been lessened, and driven further and further south each season, by mass slaughterings at the hands of white hiders. They would skin the carcass, pack the tasty tongue in brine, then simply leave the rest to rot by the thousands in the sun. Sometimes the carrion birds overhead were so thick they blocked out the sun.

For two sleeps Touch the Sky rode on. The land grew more bleak and less varied as he bore first east, then southeast, trying to spot a familiar mountain or other landmark.

He encountered enough water. But now the grass grew thinner and less nourishing, and he worried about graze for his hungry pony. For himself he managed to find and boil a few bitterroots. In the open vastness he robbed the caches of field mice for their stores of wild peas.

Never did he tarry long in one spot. He knew the Pawnee were tracking him like shadows stalk the sun. And unlike him, they had the advantage of their star charts for night travel.

By the third day after he'd survived his wound crisis, Touch the Sky was dizzy and weak with hunger. Occasional stands of forest yielded sweet acorns, a handful of green wild plums, a bit of honey. Once fortune was with him and a scrawny prairie chicken crossed his path. He killed it with his throwing ax and ate the tough, stringy meat with enjoyment, sorry it was only a few mouthfuls.

The fire to cook the bird was his first in several sleeps. Fear of the Pawnee restricted him to cold camps only. Always now, when he rested or slept, he kept his knife and bow at hand. Always he kept his back to a tree or rock, covering all approaches.

Eventually, when there was no sign he was being followed, Touch the Sky began to relax on that count. Had the lice-eaters supped full of him and the trouble he caused? Had they finally given up, assuming he must be dead?

Perhaps. But as he slogged ever onward, driving his reluctant, hungry pony, he couldn't help wondering: What did it matter if he'd eluded his enemies? Wouldn't it have been better to die fighting than to crawl to a slow, agonizing death on the open plains?

Better to die as a warrior than to die as he had so far lived: alone and belonging nowhere.

Chapter Eight

By the time Touch the Sky spotted the pony soldiers, it was too late to flee.

The midday sun burned hot and glaring from a
sky of such a deep, bottomless blue it made him
squint. He was crossing barren flats, a short-grass
prairie broken by the occasional stand of scrub
oak. He had dismounted to cautiously examine a
long-deserted white outpost.

It was a group of sod houses with long roots
trailing down from the roofs. They had been built
in a circle for defense from Indians. The walls were
loopholed to accommodate rifle barrels. A stone
watering trough in the yard held several inches
of rain.

Touch the Sky guessed that this had once served
as a way station for the white man's huge, mule-
team freight wagons. These were more and more
numerous on the plains as the "Indian menace"

meant more and more supplies for the Bluecoat army.

Little remained behind now. Touch the Sky found only some empty wooden crates and a pile of buffalo bones, all heaped in one corner of the largest sod house.

Hunger gnawed at his belly. First he turned his pony loose to graze the sparse grass of the yard and drink from the trough. Then he hauled some of the bones outside into the sunlight.

Touch the Sky cracked them open on the edge of the water trough. Then he used the point of his knife to gouge out the soft, nutritious marrow. What couldn't be reached with his blade he dug out with the point of a narrow stick.

This put little in his empty belly. But even that little bit rallied him. Now he thought of a trick Black Elk had taught his band of young warriors.

He debated. It might be risky. But it seemed so empty out here, it ought to be safe. He had seen it work once before in country such as this.

And if the Pawnee were tracking him, it hardly mattered—by now they knew exactly where he was.

Moving gingerly to accommodate his still-sore wound, Touch the Sky stacked some of the crates near the corner of one of the sod buildings. Then he climbed up and jabbed the stone point of his battle lance into the roof. Now the long red streamers flapped in the breeze.

Black Elk had thus attracted and shot a curious elk on the open plains, first tying a cloth to a stick. Perhaps, thought Touch the Sky, it would attract game now.

But instead of game, it attracted a Bluecoat cavalry squad.

Hours had passed with no luck. He gave up and was on the verge of whistling for his pony. Suddenly, a flock of frightened sparrow hawks shot by overhead.

Touch the Sky scrambled back up to the roof, careful not to skyline himself, and spotted the patrol. They rode out of the east in a fanned-out wedge formation, about a dozen strong. They were closing rapidly on the sod houses.

Outrunning them on his tired pony was out of the question. Even if he fled now, he would still be clearly visible on the open plain to the west when they reached the yard.

It was unlikely they had yet noticed the gray—she was blocked from sight by one of the sod houses. Touch the Sky whistled for her. When she trotted over, he led her behind the largest building. He could only hope the Bluecoats would make a quick check and ride on.

Otherwise . . . he slid his throwing ax out of his pannier. Otherwise, he had the element of surprise—at least one long-knife would go under with him. He had no doubt the soldiers would kill him. A Cheyenne this far from the Powder River homeland was considered a renegade. The talking papers called "treaties" had done nothing to soften the white man's heart.

It was then that Touch the Sky spotted the skunk.

It emerged from under a rocky mound near the yard, moving at the slow, leisurely pace of an animal that knows it need not bother running if threatened. Touch the Sky knew the foul-smelling secretion of its anal pouches could be whiffed from an hour's ride away. Clothing sometimes retained the stink permanently.

He had little time to consider his idea. Instead, he hurried across the yard, "attacking" the skunk.

The animal glanced back at him, then raised its long, thickly haired tail in warning. Steeling himself, keeping the wind at his back, Touch the Sky moved in closer.

The skunk turned its back, erected its tail, and began the forceful muscular contractions that shot forth the pale yellow spray. As it emptied its pouches, Touch the Sky hurriedly backed away. But still, even with the wind at his back, the powerful stink tickled his gag reflex and made tears spring to his eyes.

For a moment the wind shifted, seeming to swirl directionless. Then it steadied to a swift breeze blowing out of the southwest. As Touch the Sky, still gagging, eyes streaming, staggered back to his hidden pony, the overwhelming stench was wafted out across the plains.

The soldiers bore down on the way station, their sabers gleaming in the sun.

Their horses' iron-shod hooves tore out clumps of dirt and grass and flung them into the sky. The officer riding at the head of the wedge formation raised his saber. Now the men closed ranks and formed a skirmish line.

For a moment the sun was blocked, and Touch the Sky got a good look at the officer's face. His blood ran cold when he recognized that sneer of cold command—Lieutenant Seth Carlson!

Of course it made sense that he would encounter his old enemy this far north. Touch the Sky's soldier friend, Tom Riley from Fort Bates, had explained it. After Touch the Sky helped his white parents defeat Hiram Steele and Carlson, the officer had been reassigned to a desolate outpost up north.

Now Touch the Sky recalled his vow from that time he had refused to kill Carlson because it was nighttime, when killing should be avoided: that they would meet again by day, and that Touch the Sky would dangle the soldier's scalp from his clout.

Perhaps he would never live to dangle it, thought Touch the Sky. But if he was quick he could at least scalp his enemy before the soldiers killed him in turn.

Carlson's patrol thundered closer.

Touch the Sky slid his knife out of its sheath and gripped it in his teeth, ready. He gripped his throwing ax and watched from behind the largest house, peering cautiously around the corner.

The soldiers raised a triumphant shout as they drew closer, their blood up for adventure.

Touch the Sky quietly sang the Cheyenne Death Song even as he prepared to fight for his life. Clearly, his ruse with the skunk had been a foolish, desperate plan.

Suddenly he felt invisible fingers lift his hair: The wind had increased.

Abruptly, the noxious stink slapped the soldiers and their mounts in the face with the force of a punch.

Carlson didn't need to signal a halt. As one, the Bluecoats reined in their mounts. Two horses shied violently, one soldier leaned sideways from his saddle and retched.

It was an unwritten law of the frontier: Neither man nor beast challenged the skunk. The Bluecoats were no exception. After a hasty conference, one of them uncased a pair of field glasses. He quickly took a final look at the streamered lance.

Then Carlson barked out a command, and they rode on to the north.

Touch the Sky gave thanks to Maiyun. But even as he rode on, bearing southeast, stomach cramping from hunger, he couldn't help wondering: Had he once again eluded a quick death only to suffer a slow one?

He was no longer aware of the passing of time. By sheer force of habit, he rode when the sun was up, stopped when the last rays bled from the sky.

By now the gnawing hunger had become a part of him. He could not think of a time when he had not felt it. His cheekbones, always pronounced, now protruded like the cheeks of a skeleton. His ribs were as gaunt as barrel staves.

From time to time he encountered green plums and serviceberries. He knew that some Indians would eat any insects they could find. The Cricket Eaters, or Digger tribe, could survive indefinitely on dried ants and their larvae. But when he dug a handful out of an anthill and tried to swallow some, he only retched it all back up.

For long periods now his mind wandered as if through dream time. Again in memory he saw Honey Eater stepping out of Black Elk's tipi, wearing her beaded bride-shawl. He saw Kristen Steele, her hair like spun-gold sunshine, waiting for him in the secret copse where they used to meet.

Both gone, dead to him now. Two women from two different worlds—neither of which would let him be free.

Another moon, another sun, another hungry ride while cobwebs of delirium tangled his thoughts. At some point he had begun cutting off the buckskin strings of his fringed leggings, slowly chewing them for their meager nourishment.

Another sleep passed, and this time it was difficult to rise and get going.

He was thoroughly lost, thoroughly hungry, thoroughly dispirited. As he trudged up a long rise in the late-afternoon sun, his hand drifted to the obsidian blade of his knife.

He could fall on his knife now, and end it all quickly. The Cheyenne tribe did not consider suicide cowardly. In fact, a warrior who fell on his own knife to avoid suffering an unclean or undignified death was considered brave and was welcomed in the Land of Ghosts.

He topped the rise. Stopped. Stared long and hard, his jaw slacking open.

Suddenly, like sun bursting forth from rain-drenched heavens, Touch the Sky felt new hope surge within him. Below, reflecting silver in the glare, was a winding river swollen from rain and runoff. A choke point had formed at a sharp bend in the river, a spot where debris formed a powerful barrier.

But this was not, Touch the Sky realized, just a river. Now he knew he was somehow on the right path to Medicine Lake—and that a major vision awaited him there. For this twisting, winding river was also the horse-devouring "snake" of his recent dreams—among the objects snared by the choke point were several dead mustangs!

Chapter Nine

"Even if he is riding as slow as an old squaw," said Swift Canoe, "he should have arrived by now."

Wolf Who Hunts Smiling nodded. "Perhaps Arrow Keeper gave him special instructions which have delayed him."

"Or perhaps," said Swift Canoe, disappointment keen in his voice, "some enemy has done our work for us."

The two youths had made a camp high in the thickly wooded hills considered the center of the Cheyenne world. Below them, Medicine Lake reflected a deep blue in the morning sun. Only an occasional breeze wrinkled the mirror-smooth surface of the water. From here they could see down to the barren plains below.

While they spoke, Wolf Who Hunts Smiling had been examining the bark of a pine tree. High up in the tree, well beyond the Cheyenne's reach, the

Judd Cole

bark had been clawed deep. This was true for trees all around the lake, he'd noticed. Wolf Who Hunts Smiling recognized the marks: It was the way a grizzly bear marked its territory and warned competitors away.

All bears were wanderers, but the grizzly covered more territory than most. This bear might be nearby or clear across the hills. Wolf Who Hunts Smiling needed to know—the powerful grizzly was impossible to bring down with arrows or even most rifles. And its long, vicious claws made it the king of frontier predators. He had once seen a grizzly bring down a horse by hamstringing it with one swipe of its paws.

But the Cheyenne was not just worried about their own safety. He also had a plan hatching—assuming Touch the Sky ever arrived.

"Come," he said to Swift Canoe. "We will check our snares for rabbits. Then we will circle the lake in case our fox slipped in during the night."

Today luck was with them. They had made their way down to the lake, leapfrogging from tree to tree. As Wolf Who Hunts Smiling bent at the water's edge to drink, he spotted them off to his right: a set of long, narrow tracks made by an animal that had five toes and walked by setting its heel on the ground like a man.

Grizzly tracks. And they were fresh, judging from the dampness still trapped inside them.

"Brother," he said in a low voice to Swift Canoe, "move carefully and quietly. Do *not* let the wind slip behind you."

Like the buffalo, the grizzly had weak eyesight but a keen sense of smell. In fact it was this keen sense of smell which Wolf Who Hunts Smiling

82

had counted on when forming his plan.

A child could have followed the signs. Besides the huge prints, they encountered several ravaged places where the bear had ripped up stumps to lick up the ants underneath. They soon began to hear the crashing of tree limbs and undergrowth, the occasional deep woofing grunts. They emerged cautiously from behind a deadfall and Wolf Who Hunts Smiling raised his head.

"Stay where you are, brother," he whispered, "or sing the Death Song!"

But Swift Canoe needed no warning. Below them, reigning alone and supreme in a small clearing, was the largest, most ferocious-looking grizzly they had ever seen. It was a male, half again as high as the tallest Cheyenne in the tribe. It must have easily matched the weight of two fat ponies.

Even as they watched, the huge, brownish-yellow monster raked its mark high on the bark of a tree. The grizzly was dish-faced, high in the shoulders. The white tips of its fur looked like frost and gave the bear its names, grizzly and silvertip.

"Brother," said Swift Canoe, awe in his voice, "we must be careful. Brother Bear is still hungry from his long winter's sleep. I fear for our ponies."

"I have ears for this. We will smoke them in a cedar fire to disguise their smell."

But Wolf Who Hunts Smiling's face eased into a grin as his furtive, quick-darting eyes took in the grizzly's every move.

"What do you think, brother?" he said. "If Woman Face ever arrives, do you think brother bear should come around for a visit?"

Swift Canoe stared at him, comprehension slowly dawning on his face.

"But only think," said Wolf Who Hunts Smiling. "Bears are easily lured by smell when the wind is right. They can be led just as one leads a dog."

"And this way, *we* do not spill Cheyenne blood."

Wolf Who Hunts Smiling grinned again. "Yes. And if Arrow Keeper sends braves to find the body of his favorite dog, they will find only a badly mauled corpse. We can fulfill Black Elk's orders without sullying the Sacred Arrows."

Below, the grizzly sent a huge log flying into the trees with one careless swipe of its paw.

Touch the Sky watched ominous rain clouds pile up on the horizon like huge black boulders.

One part of him realized a terrible storm was coming on, that he ought to find shelter. The wind had picked up steadily, until the cottonwoods showed the light undersides of their leathery leaves. But another part of him was too exhausted and hungry to care.

His hopes had surged when he discovered the river with the dead ponies—horrible though it was, the discovery had confirmed his medicine dream. He had been convinced, then, that he was on the right course to Medicine Lake. Now, with the river long behind him, he was again lost in wide-open, unfamiliar plains.

And by now his hopes had ebbed. Had he actually even *seen* those dead horses in the river, or was it a trick of his failing mind? Or, if he had seen them, that snake-devouring-horses image was surely a false vision, placed over his eyes by enemy magic to torment him. Perhaps a Pawnee shaman was behind it, exacting revenge for the blood he had shed.

84

He slogged on, mechanically chewing on the last of his buckskin fringes. His pony limped now, and he knew he should check her hooves for lodged pebbles. But the thought kept fading before he could act on it.

Lightning suddenly spiderwebbed the sky, jagged, bone-white tines that speared down from the clouds to the earth.

A sudden wind gust almost stopped the gray's forward motion.

Thunder muttered, gathered rolling force, crack-boomed through the heavens in a thousand crashing echoes.

The first heavy raindrops hurtled downward, cold spikes that nailed the sky to the earth.

At first the wind and rain felt good, reviving some of Touch the Sky's energy. Then it began to pour down in earnest—great, gray, driving sheets of wind-lashed rain which stung his face.

Within minutes his horse was nearly mired in mud. Each hoof came up slowly, making wet sucking noises as they pulled clear of the mud.

She stumbled, slipped, nearly went down. Touch the Sky could see nothing around him now, just the gray curtain of rain. Desperately he tried to spot some sort of sheltered place.

Purely by chance the gray practically stumbled into a small coulee. The walls had been eroded back by wind and time, providing some shelter. Perhaps, had he been more clearheaded, Touch the Sky would have thought better of taking such low ground in this heavy rain. But all he wanted was to get somewhere where he could open his eyes again.

If anything, the force of the rain increased after

he and the gray had pressed in tight against one wall of the coulee. Only spray reached them here, driven on the wind gusts.

When he first heard a new sound of rumbling, Touch the Sky thought it was more thunder gathering.

Then, when it grew steadily louder, vibrating the ground, he thought of the rock slide which had buried the Pawnee. Only when it was too late did he realize he was about to be engulfed by a flash flood.

A huge, foaming-white gout of water swept around a turn just ahead of him in the coulee. It bore down on him with inexorable speed and power, allowing him no time to run.

It felt like a powerful fist pummeling his head when the water slammed into him. It lifted Touch the Sky and his pony like debris and swept them along the coulee. The Cheyenne saw the sky and the walls of the coulee all tumbling together, felt himself bobbing along like the floater stick of an underwater beaver trap.

The next moment, his head slammed into a boulder and Touch the Sky's world went black.

As he lay, balanced on a narrow pinnacle between life and death, he experienced another strange medicine vision.

He heard women's voices singing. At first the words were not clear. Then, slowly, he became aware that the women were singing a Cheyenne battle song.

Now the blackness gave way to flickering firelight, a huge fire like those used for clan gatherings. Now Touch the Sky saw a circle of women, Cheyenne women, young and old.

Only, he couldn't actually see them—not their faces. For while they sang, their voices raised in stirring harmony, they kept their faces hidden behind huge eagle-feather fans.

That was the last thing Touch the Sky remembered: huge fans so like the eagle's wings, flapping steadily, mysteriously, rhythmically.

Chapter Ten

His eyes eased open and then immediately closed to slits against the merciless sun.

Touch the Sky felt a fierce, throbbing pain in his right temple. He raised his hand and felt the puffy bruise that had swollen his right eye nearly shut.

He groaned as he sat up, pain coursing through him. He lay beside a huge boulder at the wide end of the coulee. The flood water had receded, leaving the rocky floor of the coulee polished and clean.

Suddenly he recalled everything that had happened. His heart leaping into his throat, he whistled for his pony.

Obediently, she trotted out from behind a rock spur to his left. Mud coated her legs and belly, and a small cut marred the coat above her left foreleg. Otherwise, she had apparently weathered the flash flood well.

Touch the Sky sat where he was, too weak and dispirited to move just yet. He was light-headed with hunger, and the gnawing complaint in his belly had become a steady, sharp pain.

As he sat there, eyes focused dully ahead of him, he became aware of a huge shadow which steadily circled the place where he sat.

Touch the Sky glanced up and saw, backlit against the sun, a magnificent eagle with a huge wingspan.

Immediately his skin goose-pimpled as he recalled his medicine vision featuring Cheyenne maidens with their faces hidden behind eagle-feather fans. Surely this was just coincidence. But Touch the Sky rarely spotted eagles in the low country like this. They nested high up in the mountains, above the rimrock. Only when prey was scarce at the higher elevations would they scour the flats for food.

Why was it circling this spot? Surely there was no game in the coulee, this close to a human. And eagles never attacked people except to defend their nests.

It was odd. But the pain in his bruised head claimed his immediate attention. He rose, fighting a dizzy rush of nausea, and staggered to a nearby pool of rain water that hadn't yet drained off. He soaked his new wound in the cold water, feeling almost instant relief.

The arrow wound in his side was still stiff and sore, but the infection was gone now. Earlier Touch the Sky had pulled up some yarrow roots and pounded them into a paste, which he carried wrapped in cottonwood leaves. Now he rubbed the last of it on his wounded side.

He glanced overhead when he had finished: The eagle still circled in the same spot.

As if it were waiting for him to set out again? But that was foolish, he scolded himself.

Foolish or not—when he set out on his pony, still bearing southeast, the eagle followed them.

For most of that day, as Touch the Sky's shadow lengthened in the sun, the eagle remained circling overhead. Now even the hunger and pain could not mute Touch the Sky's growing excitement. This was not nature's usual way: The hand of the Supernatural was in this thing.

Even so, hunger threatened to soon do him in. He was so weak that it was an effort just to stay sitting on his horse. A stab of guilt lanced through him as he recalled older Cheyenne telling stories of the times, during the short white days of the cold moons, when the tribe had slaughtered their horses for meat. Even if he could bring himself to do so, what would he do afterward? How would he survive out here without a pony?

Thus ruminating, he was slow to realize that for the first time the eagle had stopped following him. It had veered off to the right behind a slight spine of hills.

Touch the Sky halted his pony, watching it.

Had he been wrong, then? Was this after all just an oddity and not part of his vision?

If so, why did the eagle now return and then once again fly back behind the spine—as if telling him to ride that way?

Touch the Sky swerved to the right and circled around to the opposite side of the spine. As soon as he rounded the last hill, he spotted it: a wickiup, a style of hut used by various Southwest Indian tribes. It was an oval-shaped frame of branches covered with brush. They were temporary shelters, used by hunters and scouts. This far north, it could well have been built by scouts who were looking for wild horses, which were more scarce in the deserts and semiarid flats to the south.

Clearly it was old and long deserted. Forced to summon strength to do so, Touch the Sky dismounted and walked closer to investigate. The wickiup was empty.

The eagle circled patiently overhead.

Puzzled, Touch the Sky looked up at the bird, then down again at the abandoned hut. If it had led him here, why?

The eagle deviated from its pattern to swoop low over the top of a lone cottonwood behind the hut. Touch the Sky walked over to the tree and glanced up into the branches.

He squinted. There appeared to be something hanging from a limb well past the fork in the trunk.

Summoning strength he was sure he no longer possessed, he shinnied up the tree to investigate. He discovered a tough elkskin pouch which had been tied to the limb. When he opened it, he realized why: It was a generous cache of dried venison!

Indians commonly cached food during good times, often for larger groups which planned to follow them or to ensure food for their return trip. Touch the Sky was far too grateful to spend much time wondering how the meat got there. First he gave thanks to Maiyun and the four directions. Then, even before he climbed down, he tore into one of the hunks of dried meat.

Later, as he continued his journey while the eagle still followed overhead, Touch the Sky thought long and hard about the mulberry-colored birth-mark hidden in his hair and Arrow Keeper's epic vision.

He thought too about the time when he and Little Horse had been riding back to the tribe after their fight against Hiram Steele and Seth Carlson in Big-horn Falls. Just as Touch the Sky had bent to pick up a scrap of ribbon Kristen Steele had dropped, an arrow had missed him by inches.

Brother, Little Horse had said, his voice reverent with wonder, *that arrow should have put you under. But you were not meant to die just then because the hand of the Supernatural is in this thing.*

Could it be? thought Touch the Sky. Could Arrow Keeper and Little Horse be right? It still seemed impossible that he had been selected to fulfill tribal destiny.

But if he were not fate's deputy, thought the young Cheyenne as he again glanced overhead at the eagle, what was the meaning of all this?

"He was here, but not for long," said the Pawnee brave named Gun Powder. "No fire was made, and there are no droppings. Also, he is starving—see here where he cracked old buffalo bones open to eat the marrow."

Gun Powder rose from his crouch. He pointed out across the plains to the southeast, behind the sod-house complex.

"Once again, like a bird following the ancient migration route, he has gone in this direction. He is lost, but he knows where he wants to be."

"We will not let him escape us by starving," said Red Plume with conviction. "That is too easy."

"He makes no attempt to cover his signs," said

Gun Powder. "He believes we have given up the chase."

Now the brave named Short Buffalo spoke, though with difficulty. His words were slurred, the result of his still-swollen tongue and ravaged mouth—the work of the Cheyenne arrow which pierced his cheeks. As he stared toward the fugitive's escape route, his eyes were smoky with rage.

"Red Plume spoke true words. We will *not* let him starve! Place my words close to your hearts, warriors. May I die of the yellow vomit if this Cheyenne dog eludes us again! Short Buffalo will use his guts for tipi ropes!"

Only four from the original Pawnee band remained—Red Plume, Gun Powder, Iron Knife, and Short Buffalo. After the rock slide, they had used their mirrors and their lookouts to flash messages back to the main group, now waiting below the Niobrara River. Braves had been sent to collect the dead Scalp Cane and the wounded Roan Bear, whose crushed legs meant a travois had to be built. Short Buffalo, whose face and mouth had been nearly ruined by the arrow, insisted he was well enough after two sleeps' rest to accompany them again. Another five braves had joined their original group.

"If he is lost," said Red Plume, "and wounded and starving, he is as good as gone under. Ride quickly! Pawnee blood has been shed by our enemy. If he dies before we kill him, we are shamed!"

For the rest of that day the eagle flew slowly overhead, leading Touch the Sky across the vast, unfamiliar plains.

He had finally begun to recognize familiar landmarks. Those three mountain peaks which rose from the horizon like a trio of lone sentries: They were called the Three Sisters. He recognized them from the days when Black Elk led him there for warrior training.

When, near sunset, the eagle swung due east, Touch the Sky did not hesitate to follow. Exhausted, he made a simple cold camp beside an old buffalo wallow. He ate several strips of the nourishing dried venison. Then he rolled into his robe and slept a deep, dreamless sleep.

The eagle was still there in the morning, circling, patiently waiting.

Finally, when his shadow was long in front of him, Touch the Sky drew near to the eerie, darkly forested humps of the Black Hills. Night had already fallen, and the eagle was a mere shape against the blue-black sky when the young Cheyenne reached the shores of a remote, high-altitude lake.

A three-quarter moon and a fiery explosion of stars made luminous silver light reflect off the water like pale mist. He could hear the eerie cry of loons out on the lake. Touch the Sky had been here only once before in his life. But he was sure this was sacred Medicine Lake—site of Arrow Keeper's original vision, the same vision the younger Cheyenne had come to seek.

When he thought to look again, the eagle was gone.

Touch the Sky thanked Maiyun and the directions of the wind.

Then he tethered his pony in a lush patch of graze, using a long strip of rawhide to give her enough play to reach the water. Tomorrow, he reminded himself with guilt, he would inspect each foot—

hoof, pastern, and fetlock—carefully. The gray was limping steadily now. She needed rest, good forage. At least white men, he thought, could reward a good pony with a nose bag full of oats.

For a moment, as he unleashed his belongings from the gray, she shied nervously. She had seemed skittish since arriving; once, as they neared the lake, she had hunkered on her hocks and refused to move. He had been forced to dismount and gently persuade her until she moved again.

At first, bone weary himself, pain throbbing in his injured side and bruised head, he had assumed his pony was simply ill-tempered from exhaustion and her limp. Now, though, as the cry of loons echoed behind him, he too sensed some dangerous presence in this seemingly pristine and uninhabited area.

He scratched his pony's withers until she had calmed again. But as he did so, he looked cautiously all around him, watching for firelight or movement. However, all appeared well.

Now, as his uncle the moon crept toward his zenith, he searched for a safe campsite. Once again Fate seemed to treat him as a favorite child: After very little searching he found a small, dry, apparently long-deserted cave, judging from the unbroken brush crowding the entrance. It was located well back from the shoreline.

He used his knife and a piece of flint to start a small fire just inside the cave's entrance. This was not for cooking or warmth, but to explore the cave before he decided to stay there.

Good—the flickering yellow-orange light revealed no recent prints inside the cave, animal or human. The cave had a fairly wide, high entrance.

But it quickly narrowed at the back into a tiny, constricted space where he had to kneel.

Convinced it was deserted, he gathered plenty of wood and kindling and brought it inside. The well-lit night sky, and an ample supply of dry aspen and birch limbs, simplified his task.

He hauled his weapons and buffalo robe inside. Exhausted though he was, he was not yet ready to sleep. His quiver held an extra supply of arrow shafts he had cut from a dead pine. Now, in the wavering firelight, he carefully honed the shafts and hardened the points in the fire.

Soon, the grueling ordeal of invoking the medicine dream must begin. The Pawnee were only at the back of his mind now. He was sure they had given up on tracking him—how much could one Cheyenne buck be worth to them?

True, he reminded himself, he had shed Pawnee blood, and all Plains tribes placed a high value on vengeance. But if they had wanted him, surely they would have killed him long before this.

Still, even as his eyelids finally grew heavy with sleep, a quick lance of foreboding stabbed through him. He suddenly had the feeling that human eyes were watching him from behind the dark cloak of the night.

Once again he stepped outside, watching and listening to the night. But nothing seemed amiss.

Chiding himself for a white-livered coward, he got a firm purchase on his courage. Then he stepped back into the cave.

Chapter Eleven

"Wake up," said Wolf Who Hunts Smiling. "Today we kill our enemy!"

Swift Canoe rolled out of his buffalo robe, instantly wide awake despite the lopsided shape of his sleepy face. He remembered the night before, watching every move when Touch the Sky had arrived and made his camp.

Most Indians were late sleepers. In order to rise with the sun, Wolf Who Hunts Smiling had drunk much water the night before so his aching bladder would rouse him.

"He should sleep long yet," said Swift Canoe. "He was exhausted when he arrived. Did you see his ribs protrude?"

Wolf Who Hunts Smiling nodded.

"True, he is weak from hunger. But count little on this. Though I hate and despise him, I admit Woman Face is strong and capable. We must work quickly and be careful."

"I am more worried about Brother Bear than Woman Face," said Swift Canoe. "We might easily lure him to *us* instead. Should we not after all do this thing ourselves?"

"This is no time to show the brains of a rabbit," said Wolf Who Hunts Smiling impatiently. "Recall, if our plan works, *we* do not sully the Sacred Arrows by drawing Cheyenne blood. Too, Arrow Keeper will surely send someone to find Woman Face. This way they will find mauled remains, and we will not be suspected. Not all in the tribe believed Black Elk's story that we were sent out to scout Pawnee."

"I have ears for this. But if the plan does not work'?"

Wolf Who Hunts Smiling's dark, furtive eyes met his friend's. "If the plan does not work, we kill him ourselves."

They were camped high on a thickly wooded hillside behind Medicine Lake. The sun had not yet risen, and the early morning sky was still the color of flint. The sweet song of the larks greeted them as they set out toward a tall cedar located halfway between their camp and the shore of the lake.

They had already selected this tree because, from its top branches, one could see the entire area all the way down to the plains. From this tree they had discovered the grizzly's den and some of the creature's favorite hunting routes.

When they reached the tree, Wolf Who Hunts Smiling quickly climbed to the top. The sun was starting to rise from her birthplace, and far below on the flats he saw prairie falcons circling, hunting for squirrels.

Closer at hand, all was quiet at the entrance to Touch the Sky's cave. And further, past the far end of the lake, it was also quiet near the rocky entrance to the grizzly's den.

Wolf Who Hunts Smiling was patient. All bears were early risers when not in hibernation. He watched every spot where he had seen the grizzly prowling, looking for movement, not shape.

Finally he spotted it. The huge silvertip had torn open an anthill. He was letting the ants run up his paw before he licked them off. This way the bear avoided sand and stickers. Each time its tongue shot out, Wolf Who Hunts Smiling saw large, sharp canines.

At first the Cheyenne's heart sank. The wind was to the grizzly's back, blowing away from the entrance to Touch the Sky's cave.

But then the grizzly began ambling toward the opposite shore of the lake, into the face of the wind.

Wolf Who Hunts Smiling nimbly climbed back down to the ground.

"Quickly!" he told Swift Canoe. "Now we follow our plan!"

Two sleeps earlier they had located a deer run which led to the shore of the lake. Every morning whitetail deer came down to the water to drink. The two Cheyenne had already constructed a blind of dead brush and limbs.

They slipped quietly up to their hiding place and peeked around it toward the lake. A doe and her fawn were drinking.

Wolf Who Hunts Smiling had recently made a strong new bow from oak. Now he pulled an arrow from his quiver and slid the string into the notch.

The doe stepped a few paces into the clear water and her fawn followed. Wolf Who Hunts Smiling remembered Black Elk's lesson: Always try to shoot game when it's in the water. That way, if the first bullet or arrow doesn't kill it, its escape will be slowed so the second shot can bring it down.

But he needed no second shot. His first arrow pierced the fawn's soft flank and struck warm vitals, dropping it in the water. The startled doe was gone in several quick bounds.

Quickly the two Cheyenne hauled the fawn ashore. Swift Canoe unsheathed his bone-handle knife and opened the fawn up from throat to rump. Meantime, Wolf Who Hunts Smiling climbed the lookout tree again to make sure the grizzly was still downwind.

It was.

They dragged the bleeding fawn to a high ridge located between Touch the Sky's cave and the prowling grizzly. The wind, a stiff, steady breeze, was directly behind them now.

From this high ground they could see the huge, yellow-brown grizzly, though the nearly blind bear could not possibly spot them. They watched it rise, sniff the air, then stand rooted as the breeze wafted the smell of the bleeding fawn.

"Brother," said Swift Canoe triumphantly, "he has fixed on the smell. And have you ever seen a bear this huge?"

"Hurry!" said Wolf Who Hunts Smiling as the dish-faced monster began lumbering toward them.

Lugging the bloody carcass between them, they raced back toward the entrance of Touch the Sky's cave. Wolf Who Hunts Smiling drew another arrow, ready to kill him if they woke him up. But they managed to leave the fawn just inside the dark cave entrance without alarming the sleeping Cheyenne within.

Then they raced away like a pair of scalded dogs, heading for the safe vantage point of their camp.

"Brother," said Wolf Who Hunts Smiling, "it is like stealing eggs from a nest on the ground."

"True. The very sight of Brother Bear at his cave entrance will turn Woman Face Wendigo!"

Once again Touch the Sky slept a deep, dreamless sleep as his body regained some of its depleted strength.

But at first, when a deep, angry bellow woke him like a kick to the face, he was convinced he was indeed dreaming: A gigantic grizzly, its curved claws dripping gobbets of bloody meat, nearly filled the entrance to the cave!

Touch the Sky had placed his robe near the back of the cave. Now he reflexively pressed even tighter against the wall, his heart leaping into his throat.

He spotted the fawn, now tossed aside in the bear's rage as it encountered the overpowering smell of a human. Perhaps it had intended to cache it here. Had the Cheyenne, after all, mistakenly selected a bear's den?

But that was impossible, he thought—there had been no smells or other obvious signs of animal occupation. And though they were still early in the warm moons, it was too late for a grizzly to be emerging from its hibernation-like sleep.

Still—clearly this one was mean and ravenous as a bear waking from its winter sleep. Many grizzlies had experience with white hunters and had come to hate humans. Now, as this one pressed even closer to the frightened Cheyenne, Touch the Sky spotted a gnarled scar where a bullet had caught the bear high on the chest.

Touch the Sky's scalp was sweating, fear had turned his limbs to stone. A paw swiped past his face, only inches away. He knew those hard-as-steel claws could rip a horse open in one swipe.

Again the grizzly's angry bellow, another pass of the lethal claws. The wind from the near miss fanned Touch the Sky's face. He could smell the bear's stinking breath every time it bellowed.

Luckily, however, the cave was apparently too small as it tapered toward the rear. Touch the Sky felt a little strength returning to his limbs as this fact sank in. The grizzly could fit only its head, forelegs, and part of its high shoulders past the entrance.

But clearly he was trapped here so long as the bear chose to remain.

Desperately he eyed his weapons. As always, he had slept with them close to hand. But his bow would be useless in such tight quarters, he didn't even have room to draw the string back. His throwing ax and knife would be equally useless, like attacking Bluecoat artillery with rocks.

Besides—a grizzly was almost impossible to kill without a huge-bore rifle.

The bear grunted as it squeezed even tighter into the entrance. Its eyes were charged with blood lust.

102

The claws barely missed him this time. On the second swipe, they caught the edge of the buffalo robe and shredded it.

Touch the Sky pressed flat against the cool stone wall of the small cave. The smell of the grizzly was overpowering, its breath hot and moist on his bare skin.

He tried to fight down his panic so he could think. Now he recalled Arrow Keeper's stories about Cheyenne who had made medicine talk to animals, taming them and even becoming their friends in the wild.

"Brother Bear," he said, his voice calm and friendly, "I am a red man! It was white hunters who tried to put you under and left that hurt on your skin. The red man lives like his brother the bear, wild and hunted, safe nowhere!"

The grizzly quieted, as if the Cheyenne words were a strange but soothing music.

"Brother Bear! Why kill me? Look at my lean body—I am stringy and tough from hunger, like winter-starved game. The tender meat on that fawn will be better in your belly."

Suddenly, however, his voice seemed to further enrage the grizzly. This time one set of claws actually took a nick out of his right knee, sending a burning pain up his leg.

Touch the Sky fell silent, hoping to simply outwait the bear. But though it eventually backed out of the cave, it refused to leave the entrance. Periodically, it would suddenly become enraged and thrust its way back in, hoping to catch the Cheyenne in a careless moment.

This went on for some time. Outside, the sun rose higher and sent more light into the cave. Touch the Sky's back and legs were severely cramped from the long crouch against the back wall. He knew he could not maintain this position much longer without pushing his tired, weak muscles to collapse.

And the only way to fall was forward, into the bear's claws.

Better to take a lesson from Black Elk's warrior training: When attacked and all seems lost, become the aggressor, not the victim.

He had been eyeing the pile of kindling and wood for some time. Like his weapons, it lay close to hand. The plan he had in mind was dangerous—might in fact very well kill him. But it was the only hope he saw.

Each time the grizzly backed out of the cave, Touch the Sky would hurriedly draw wood and kindling close. And each time he did so, the bear in turn bellowed in fury and thrust back into the cave. So it took the Cheyenne quite some time to assemble enough material for a fire.

He struck a spark from his flint and ignited a pile of kindling. Then he piled on wood. During all this the bear continually tried to rip him with its slashing claws. Twice they tossed burning wood from the fire; each time the Cheyenne threw it back in.

There was enough air for a fire, but no ventilation for the heat and smoke. Tears sprang to Touch the Sky's eyes as smoke billowed into them. The heat singed his skin and he coughed hard, wracking coughs as acrid fingers of smoke and heat tickled his lungs.

The bear too coughed. Then, as more and more smoke accumulated, it backed out of the cave.

Now, thought Touch the Sky.

Pulling his shredded robe out from under him, he brought it down over the fire for a moment, lifted it until the flames leaped up again, then brought it down again. He was making a smudge fire like the kind used to chase off mosquitoes.

Huge black clouds of smoke billowed from the cave entrance now. Gagging, his eyes streaming, Touch the Sky heard the enraged beast bellow as it backed further away. If only he could hang on a little longer, he told himself, make a little more smoke . . .

Outside, the wind suddenly shifted. A moment later the thick pall of smoke was sucked back into the cave.

It caught Touch the Sky flush and pressed the last breath of air out of the cave. He could see nothing through the tears streaming from his eyes. All he knew was that he was suffocating. Now there was no question of hanging on a bit longer, now it no longer mattered where the bear was. Either he got out or he died of suffocation.

Deciding to take his chance with the bear, he screamed the Cheyenne war cry to nerve himself.

Then, the Death Song on his lips, he sprang forward through the entrance to the cave.

Chapter Twelve

"Look!"

The Pawnee brave named Gun Powder pointed south across the empty plain. The sun was still new on the eastern horizon to his left, a dull yellow ball without warmth. In the direction he pointed, the Black Hills were just now starting to take form against the skyline.

The newborn sun provided enough light to make the dark, puffy clouds visible as they rose above the hills like escaping bubbles.

"Smoke! We have no lookouts this far east," said Red Plume, their battle chief. "They cannot be made by our messengers."

"This is not talking smoke," said Gun Powder with conviction. "No tribe uses such signals. Our fox has carelessly built a fire and revealed his den."

"*I* am for Cheyenne blood!" said Short Buffalo,

thrusting his battle lance high.

Though his words were brave, they were badly muffled because of his wounded mouth. Several braves were forced to turn their heads to hide their wry smiles.

"Scalp Cane gave me ponies after the Apache stole my clan's herds," said Iron Knife. "Now he has crossed over unclean thanks to this Cheyenne buck. Roan Bear has only nineteen winters behind him. But he will never walk straight like a man again, his legs are so twisted. I will *drink* this Cheyenne's blood, not merely smear it on my face!"

"You do well to speak in a kill-cry," said Red Plume to Iron Knife, contempt clear in his tone. "You, the eagle-eyed brave who missed a pony's rump with his arrow!"

Several other warriors laughed. Rage smoked in Iron Knife's eyes, but he set his face one way and held it, ignoring the others and looking only at Red Plume.

"In the Medicine Bonnet clan, we are taught that a good Crow pony is worth more than a good Cheyenne buck. This one time I may have missed with my arrow. But my knife, once drawn, always strikes vitals."

The challenge was clear in his tone, and Red Plume knew Iron Knife had spoken straight. Red Plume was a good battle leader, quick on his feet and able to think clearly even when the enemy's unnerving war cry sounded. But Iron Knife was a killer to be reckoned with in a blade fight. Red Plume already regretted his harsh words just now. He also rued his promise to take back one of Iron Knife's coup feathers as punishment for his bad shot. This was no time to push the hot-tempered brave further.

"Your clan teaches wisely, then," said Red Plume. "We are Pawnee brothers of the Kitkehanki, men of men. And we are united against our enemy!"

He and Iron Knife crossed lances and the rest of the warriors raised their shrill war cry. They had ridden through much of the night, easily tracking their quarry. By now they knew he was headed for the Black Hills and the Cheyenne's sacred lake—no doubt expecting help from their God.

Short Buffalo's swollen and torn face was a constant reminder to the others of this elusive Cheyenne buck's dangerous skill. One of the new arrivals to the group, a warrior named Sun Road, had joined the Pawnee group known as the Skidi when they attacked Yellow Bear's camp one winter ago. Sun Road swore this tall buck they sought now was the same who had killed the Skidi battle leader, War Thunder.

The Pawnee warriors dug their heels and knees hard into their ponies, their minds set only on vengeance.

At first, when he burst forth from the smoke-filled maw of the cave, Touch the Sky could see nothing. His eyes ached and streamed tears, his throat and lungs cried for air. But each time he gasped, they purchased only raw, burning pain.

He dropped to the ground, helpless, choking, expecting death at any moment. But steel claws did not rip his muscles from his bones nor spill his guts in one swipe. Nor was he picked up, like a limp rag doll in a terrier's jaws, and dashed to pieces on the rocks.

Smoke was still rising in wisps behind him when Touch the Sky realized that, for now at least, the bear was gone. His eyes were still streaming and blurred. But he could see now that the grizzly was nowhere close by.

Still—he was far from safe, he reminded himself. The huge predator was no doubt still in the area around the lake. Bears were highly territorial and did not quit an area easily. Now it had even more reason than ever to hate humans.

Touch the Sky had no weapons that could bring down a grizzly. His only hope for survival lay in avoiding and outwitting the ill-tempered monster.

Finally, a cool breath bathed his aching lungs. Another.

Slowly, Touch the Sky sat up in the grass.

Across the lake, where his pony was tethered in lush graze, there was a sound like a sturdy tree limb snapping.

Across the lake . . .

. . . *where his pony was tethered!*

Touch the Sky leaped to his feet. He turned around slowly in a circle until he felt the breeze steady in his face. It was blowing from the north: meaning his pony was almost certainly downwind from the bear.

He hurried back into the cave and grabbed his bow and quiver of new arrows. Then he raced down toward the shore of the lake.

Trees grew close to the water, obscuring his view of the little sheltered cove where he'd left the gray. Touch the Sky leaped over fallen trees and gnarled roots, swerved to avoid bramble thickets and boulders.

Another tree limb snapped, leaves were violently shaken.

A sudden, frightened nicker was followed by an angry bellow.

Too late!

Desperation sent more strength surging into Touch the Sky's legs. His wounded side protested with a jolt of pain each time he leaped a log or root.

The gray's panicked whinnying was unrelenting now. More limbs snapped, leaves rattled, the grizzly's deep bellows seemed to pulsate the air and vibrate the ground.

Touch the Sky cleared the last trees and reached the cove. On the gently sloping grassy bank, rearing at the end of its tether, the gray held the grizzly at bay with her wildly flailing hooves.

The horse's frightened nickering sounded more terrifying than the anguished cries of mortally wounded Cheyenne on a battlefield. Touch the Sky was upwind, and the bear hadn't noticed him yet. It was too intent on killing the horse.

There was nothing else Touch the Sky could do. So he slid a fire-hardened arrow from his quiver and notched it to his bowstring. There was no hope, of course, of killing or even seriously hurting the grizzly. But it had to at least be distracted—or Touch the Sky had an impossible walk ahead of him across a no-man's-land.

He took cover in a swale behind a spruce thicket.

The grizzly was not so blind that it would fail to make out his human shape at this close range.

The gray nickered, reared, kicked out with her forelegs.

The grizzly's right paw swiped. The claws raked furrows in the pony's muscle-corded chest. The bear reached back for a second, more deadly blow.

Touch the Sky let fly his arrow. It struck the grizzly's shaggy, yellow-brown fur just below the left shoulder.

The beast's surprised grunt was followed by a roar much louder than its usual woofing bellow. Enraged, but also frightened, the grizzly crashed into the trees and fled.

His pony was so terrified that Touch the Sky was forced to talk to her for a long time before he could approach her. He finally got her calmed down. Then he led her into the cool lake to bathe her new wounds. They still bled, but were not deep.

This was a bad omen, thought Touch the Sky. This sojourn to Medicine Lake had proven to be a disaster from its very beginning. He had hoped the arrival of the mysterious eagle signaled a change in his fortunes.

Now—in addition to angry Pawnee, neglected wounds, and a half-starved body—he had an enraged grizzly to contend with. Arrow Keeper had not made this mission sound so complicated and dangerous when he explained it back at camp.

Again, as Touch the Sky led his horse back out of the clean lake, he felt a cool tickle of premonition move up the bumps of his spine like a feather.

*   *   *

"I *told* you hunger would make him no less dangerous," Wolf Who Hunts Smiling said bitterly.

"Did you see how cleverly he eluded Brother Bear?" said Swift Canoe. His tone was begrudgingly respectful. "Not once did he show the white feather."

"He is a warrior," said Wolf Who Hunts Smiling. "But he is no Cheyenne! He has brought contamination to our tribe. We are bound by Black Elk's orders."

Both youths were crouched behind a hawthorn bush just down ridge from their hidden camp. The lake lay even further down below them.

"I tried to kill him once," said Swift Canoe, fitting an arrow to his string. "But he ducked just as I shot. This time I will sink my shaft into the quick of him!"

Wolf Who Hunts Smiling made no move to stop his friend. Despite his talk of Touch the Sky's being a spy, the main reason Wolf Who Hunts Smiling hated him was envy. Clearly Arrow Keeper was preparing the tall stranger for a leadership position within the tribe. But Wolf Who Hunts Smiling had his own ambitions for the tribe, and had already begun winning younger warriors over to his way of thinking. He hoped to soon form his own military society within the tribe and challenge the Headmen, who were not keen enough to take the fight to the encroaching white men.

Even so, just as Swift Canoe had eased his bowstring back, Wolf Who Hunts Smiling took his arm in a grip as strong as an eagle's talons.

"Hold, brother! Look, down on the plains!"

Swift Canoe glanced down the forested hillside, looking where his friend pointed. His jaw fell slack with surprise.

Both Cheyenne immediately recognized the distinctive topknots of the approaching riders: Pawnee! They counted nine riders, coming from exactly the same direction that Touch the Sky had chosen.

"They are tracking Woman Face," Wolf Who Hunts Smiling said with conviction.

"You must be right, brother! See how they fan out now? See how they dismount? They are hobbling their horses."

"They hope to surprise him."

"True," said Swift Canoe. "But lice-eaters will not content themselves with one kill if more Cheyenne are available."

The nervousness in Swift Canoe's tone was clear, as was his meaning. Wolf Who Hunts Smiling thought for a moment, then nodded at his companion's words.

"There are too many of them for us to fight," said Wolf Who Hunts Smiling.

"Woman Face is too far down to see them until it is too late for him. Now is the time for us to ride down the back of this hill and flee."

Wolf Who Hunts Smiling considered this. He hated to come this far, wait this long, come this close, only to flee now. But if a grizzly made an area dangerous, Pawnee made it doubly so. Staying here much longer meant that he and Swift Canoe risked capture themselves.

Judd Cole

"I have ears for your words," said Wolf Who Hunts Smiling.

His quick-darting, furtive eyes raced back and forth between the approaching Pawnee and the unsuspecting Cheyenne below. "Let us ride. A little smoke will not save Woman Face this time. Let the bloodthirsty Pawnee finish what Brother Bear has begun."

Chapter Thirteen

The Pawnee, still unaware of the grizzly's presence, silently formed a ring around Medicine Lake. Despite their proud boasts and their eagerness to seize this deadly enemy, they were warriors of the Kitkehahki branch of the Pawnee—raised near the river the whites called the Republican. They were highly disciplined fighters who valued obedience to their battle chiefs. They would wait for the signal from Red Plume before they showed themselves.

And that signal would not come yet, for Red Plume was curious.

He had already discussed this loner Cheyenne with Gun Powder, his best scout and most battle-tested brave. Gun Powder, like Red Plume and all true warriors, respected a worthy enemy. Both Pawnee agreed: This Cheyenne was on a special mission to invoke strong medicine. Strong medicine which might be turned against the Pawnee nations when they combined for the massive raid during the upcoming Cheyenne chief-renewal ceremony.

Better to find out, thought Red Plume now as he lay behind a thick oak, watching. The Cheyenne buck was clearly visible now. He was younger than Red Plume had expected—perhaps 18 or 19 winters behind him. He was tipi-pole thin with starvation and moved as if tired. But he was also tall, even for a Cheyenne, and his wide shoulders hinted at a sturdy frame when well fed.

Red Plume absently dug a louse out of the stiff grease in his topknot and cracked it between his strong white teeth. Of all the tribes he knew, the Cheyenne perhaps more than any other feared being separated from the rest of their tribe. So terrible was solitude to them that rarely would they banish even a murderer.

So whatever this one had been sent to do, it was important, thought Red Plume.

The Pawnee war chief frowned when he saw Iron Knife stick his head out too far from behind a dogwood tree. Disciplined or not, the proud warrior had been humiliated by his miss with the arrow. Now he ached to make amends by gutting this Pawnee-killer. But he would have to hurry to wrest that pleasure from the injured Short Buffalo, who had first claim to his blood.

Hold off, said the look Red Plume gave both impatient braves. *Your time approaches. For now, just watch and learn.*

His sister the sun was not yet far above the eastern horizon when Touch the Sky began constructing the willow-branch frame.

Vision Quest

You must purify yourself in the sweat lodge before you leave and again when you arrive.

Arrow Keeper's words returned in memory and guided Touch the Sky's purpose. While he worked, one ear was cocked for warnings of the bear's return. The Cheyenne knew he was still too weak to attempt the grueling ordeal of invoking a vision. This day he would sweat himself clean. Then he would paint his face, meditate, rest, and eat, regaining strength.

He bent the flexible willow branches into shape, lashed them together with buffalo-hair ropes. He returned to the cave and carried his now-tattered buffalo robe back. He draped it over the frame.

You will be on a sojourn to sacred Medicine Lake seeking a medicine dream of great consequence to the Cheyenne people.

Touch the Sky built a hot fire of aspen and oak inside the crude frame hut. One by one, he heaped rocks in a circle about the fire and let them heat for a long time. Only when they finally began to glow red did he strip out of his breechclout and leggings and moccasins.

He filled his buckskin legging sash with cold lake water, then returned to the sweat lodge. Before he lifted the hide and went inside, he paused to glance all around the lake.

He felt eyes watching him—unseen but close.

He glanced toward his pony, tethered nearby. She had calmed since the confrontation with the silvertip bear. But now she too watched the trees all around them, wary. Her ears flicked forward, listening.

You must experience the vision in all of its force at Medicine Lake. Only then can you resolve this terrible

*battle in your heart. Only then will you accept who
you are and what must be done.*

Touch the Sky went inside and dumped the cold
water on the glowing rocks. At first the hissing steam
nearly scalded him. But soon it cooled enough to
comfortably breathe. He sat cross-legged in the
swirling wisps of steam, feeling his pores expand
and ooze cleansing sweat.

He sat for a long time, until his mind was empty
of thoughts. Finally, as the rivulets of sweat began
to cool against his skin, he left the sweat lodge.

He wiped down with clumps of willow leaves,
followed this with a cooling plunge in the lake.
Then he dressed again.

Near the water he dug red-bank clay out and put
some on a piece of bark to dry a bit in the sun. He
crushed ripe blackberries and mixed the juice with
yarrow paste to make black dye. He mashed brown
wild turnip roots with blades of lush green grass,
grinding them together between rocks to produce
a yellow paint.

Touch the Sky painted his forehead yellow, his
nose red, his chin black—the Cheyenne battle colors. Warriors painted this way when making their
sacrifice to the Medicine Arrows before battle.
Touch the Sky would remain painted until he
experienced the vision—assuming he was destined
to receive it.

*But Father, what if I fail in seeking this medicine
dream?*

*You will either experience this medicine vision,
young Cheyenne warrior, or I fear you will be killed
in the attempt.*

Touch the Sky finished painting and headed back
toward the cave. Now he would eat some more

venison, then inspect his pony's hooves before he
began the final rest and meditation for his vision
quest.

Suddenly a hideous shrieking broke out all
around him.

A moment later a circle of well-armed Pawnee
braves was closing in on him, their eyes fierce
with blood lust.

"Our young fox shook the hounds for many
sleeps," said a Pawnee with a huge red plume in
his topknot. He advanced closer, speaking in the
mixture of Lakota Sioux and Northern Cheyenne
dialects he had learned from prisoners. "But now
he has led the hounds to his very den!"

He said something rapidly in Pawnee to the others and the rest stopped. Only the brave in the red
plume advanced closer toward Touch the Sky.

"I know your tribe well enough to know you are
painted for an important ceremony, I speak one
way and tell you honestly, I grew alarmed as I
watched you. If I tolerated this thing much longer,
would you succeed in bringing strong medicine
down on Cheyenne enemies? For I believe as Gun
Powder preaches: All red men worship one God
by different names. Only, the Cheyenne chose to
starve our women and children by hoarding the
buffalo! For this we war, buck! Now you have
blooded my warriors, and your blood is the price
of their souls."

"You drew first blood!" Touch the Sky retorted.
"Have the Cheyenne sold themselves to the Bluecoats as scouts to hunt down red men? Have *I*
starved a Pawnee woman or babe? Has *this*
Cheyenne fired on your elders or ever raised his

war lance against any Pawnee except in defense of his tribe?"

"He has indeed, Red Plume!" said one of the warriors who had joined Red Plume's band after the rock slide. "I fought in the raids one winter ago against Yellow Bear's camp. *This* tall buck is the one who sent War Thunder over!"

The speaker realized he had spoken the name of a dead man and now made the cut-off sign, asking forgiveness of Tirawa, the Pawnee Father.

"Do you deny this thing?" Red Plume demanded.

Touch the Sky held his mouth in a straight, determined line, showing nothing in his face. By now he had learned well the lesson of Old Knobby, the former mountain man who had befriended him in Bighorn Falls: If captured by Indians, *never* let them see your fear. Begging them for mercy only ensured a slow, agonizing death by torture.

"I deny nothing!" he said defiantly. "Once the war cry sounds, I am for greasing *any* enemy's bones with my battle paint!"

These brave words earned looks of respect from several of the warriors, including Red Plume and Gun Powder.

"I have no ears for this," said another brave. But Touch the Sky barely understood him—not only were the words unfamiliar, the Pawnee's mouth was cruelly mangled. Then the Cheyenne saw the ragged holes in both cheeks and realized this was a victim of his powerful new bow and fire-hardened arrows.

"Look!" added the wounded Pawnee. "Even now his eyes search for boulders to bring down upon us! But a woman's trickery will not save him this time."

Vision Quest

Touch the Sky's mind worked furiously. Fighting them was out of the question, as was running. Nine of them circled him, one facing him no matter where he turned. For the present, it was necessary to gain more time to hatch a plan.

"Boulders!" he said loudly, mustering scorn. "For killing Pawnee? Give me a handful of pebbles!"

"Hold, Iron Knife, or forfeit your war bonnet!"

The leader with the brilliant red plume spoke just in time to prevent a warrior from sinking his knife to the hilt in Touch the Sky. It was a French dragoon's bayonet with a deep blood gutter carved in its iron blade to facilitate rapid bleeding.

"Pebbles! For a buck who has barely left the dug, you talk the he-bear talk," said Red Plume. "Are you like a cat who spits and makes a war face but does little else?"

Touch the Sky had to do something, and quickly. The others were impatient to gain vengeance for their fallen comrades. They were clearly tiring of his blustering talk.

Invisible fingers tickled the left side of his face, and Touch the Sky realized the wind was shifting.

The wind . . .

Where was the silvertip? It had disappeared behind that long ridge north of the lake. So far, they had all been downwind, assuming it was still north of the water. But now the wind blew straight out of the south. It would carry the human smell along with the smell of their horses, hobbled below.

Despite their precise star charts and their scorn of red men who feared the dark, the Pawnee were vastly superstitious. Touch the Sky's friend Corey Robinson had once saved Yellow Bear's tribe merely by posing as a madman—Pawnee warri-

121

ors considered insane whites to be the strongest bad medicine in their world.

This was his only chance, Touch the Sky decided. A slim chance was better than a sure death.

"I know nothing of spitting cats!" he said in a brazen, challenging tone. "My name is Bear Caller. I have been sent here by my tribe's shaman because my magic is strong medicine."

"Your magic! Do you carry the famous Cheyenne bloodstone which makes your prints invisible to an enemy?"

The scorn in Red Plume's tone made several other warriors laugh.

"Not this," said one of them. "This buck knows the secret words which turn horse droppings into pemmican!"

Even Short Buffalo and Iron Knife, impatient to gut this dog, laughed at this.

The wind still blew from the south. *Hurry, Brother Bear*, thought Touch the Sky.

"I told you, I am Bear Caller. My people call me this because I am of the Bear Clan and the bear is my brother. I can summon the ferocious grizzly to kill my enemies!"

"And *I* am called Bird Follower because I can fly across the sky!" said Iron Knife. "You are like the whites, speaking many bold words which mean little."

"Summon this ferocious grizzly," said Red Plume. "Show us this strong medicine."

The wind was a steady, stiff breeze now. But had the bear moved on? thought Touch the Sky desperately.

The Pawnee mocked him mercilessly when Touch the Sky loosed an imitation of the grizzly's hungry woofing sound. He repeated it several times, a barking cough from deep in his chest.

"Oooff!" said one of the warriors, imitating their prisoner. "Oooff, ooff-ooff!"

The rest laughed so hard that one or two of them fell upon the ground.

"See how the silvertip rushes to aid his brother," said Red Plume. "Your medicine is indeed powerful."

More laughter. But at that moment the enraged bear hiding in the woods whiffed the overwhelming smell of humans and horses violating his territory. The roaring bellow it unleashed reminded Touch the Sky of buffalo bulls locked in combat.

Tree limbs crashed, there were more bellows. As one, the nine Pawnee turned to stare toward the ridge.

The monster that suddenly appeared on top of the ridge stretched out to his full height on his hind legs. He bellowed his rage, then started lumbering clumsily but with impressive speed toward the group of intruders.

Had they acted in concert, the Pawnee could have brought the grizzly down with their arrows and lances. But the one thing which could quickly destroy their battlefield discipline was strong magic. And this Cheyenne had just summoned a silvertip to his aid, right before their eyes! His magic was indeed strong—the strongest they had ever seen.

The Pawnee panicked and fled downhill toward their horses. This headlong flight distracted the bear. Touch the Sky raced toward his own pony, now rearing against her tether as the grizzly drew nearer.

Touch the Sky untied the rawhide tether and leaped onto the gray, speaking soothing words to fight her panic. Then, as the angry bear routed his enemies, he rode into the dense cover of trees.

Chapter Fourteen

Honey Eater sat just outside the entrance flap of Black Elk's tipi, watching the unmarried girls crossing camp toward their sewing lodge.

How much like fresh flowers some of them looked! And though she was as young as many of them, how much older and wearier Honey Eater felt when she watched them skipping and laughing. The tribe prepared them, almost from birth, for the great rite of passage to womanhood: marriage. And yet, who spoke of this misery and heartache she felt now?

Some of them waved to her, and the young beauty waved back, putting on the gay face that was expected of a great chief's daughter. She missed her friends from the other clans. They would spend much of their morning learning the domestic arts of the tribe from the older squaws. Much gossip and teasing would take place as the girls learned such skills as the highly prized art of Cheyenne beadwork. It was considered the finest on the plains, and the Cheyenne women jealously guarded their secrets.

Honey Eater was finishing an elk hide on pumice stone, softening it for the awl and thread. Inside, Black Elk still slept. He had been up most of the night with the rowdiest warriors, gambling and betting on pony races. He had been cold and remote with her ever since Touch the Sky had been sent on his mission by Arrow Keeper.

Touch the Sky . . . where was he?

Again she let the elkskin fall around her lap as her thoughts wandered. She had tried to be a good Cheyenne wife, to keep her mind free of thoughts for any brave except Black Elk. But she was a simple creature with only one heart—and her one heart was filled with love for the tall youth who had sworn his love for her aloud even as white devils tortured him.

Was he even alive? *Why* did he have to return from Bighorn Falls after she had given up all hope? After River of Winds made his report about Touch the Sky and the golden-haired girl he held in his blanket, she had tried to turn her heart to stone toward him.

But always, at the back of every dream, she heard his voice from that night when he was sure he was about to die: "Do you know that I have placed a stone in front of my tipi?" he had called out to her. "When that stone melts, so too will my love for you!"

The stone was still there—still unmelted. She checked every day.

It was her father's death, thought Honey Eater,

unconsciously making the cut-off sign. His passing and tribal law had left her no choice. She had only accepted Black Elk's gift of horses after Arrow Keeper reminded her. Her duty was to the tribe, and the tribe expected a chief's daughter to marry Black Elk.

The hide flap over the tipi entrance was lifted aside and Black Elk stepped outside. He was naked save for his clout. He glanced down at the unfinished hide and frowned.

"Have you made this the work of your old age, woman? I need new moccasins. Do you expect a war chief to go about looking as if he has neither meat nor racks to store it?"

"I am sorry," she said guiltily.

She stretched the elkskin tight in her fingers and began scraping it over the rough stone. Secretly, though, she was weary of this constant boasting about war. All it ever brought was pain and loss and terrible suffering. Could men find nothing else to worship?

"You dream far too much," said Black Elk. "Your thoughts are seldom on your work and your duties as a wife."

These words hung in the air between them like harsh smoke, accusing her. He had not mentioned Touch the Sky by name, but they both knew what he hinted at.

"My duties?"

She tried to keep her voice submissive as she pointed to the tripod where his elk steak waited for him, dripping succulent kidney fat. "There waits your breakfast. I have made your tea just as you like it. I have also made you new clothing for the chief-renewal. Your war bonnet is the finest in the Cheyenne nation, your horse blanket embroidered like no other. I cook your meals, rub your aching muscles, sew your new moccasins. How, then, have I neglected my duties?"

Black Elk scowled, looking fierce. His severed, dead flap of ear looked like wrinkled leather. "Do not take this tone with me! I am your husband and your war chief! If you have done your duty, then tell me you have my son in your womb."

Honey Eater averted her eyes. "I cannot catch a baby as if it were a toy thrown to me."

"No. But a cow must rut before she can become heavy with calf. You have no desire to lie with your own husband. I have felt how you pull back from my embrace. Is this what you call doing your duty?"

Honey Eater was silent. His words held some truth, and she felt her guilt. It was a Cheyenne squaw's obligation to put her husband and her tribe before her own needs. But her body rebelled against her conscience: She could not even pretend pleasure with another man so long as it was Touch the Sky she burned for.

Black Elk read the confession in her silence. Rage filled him for a moment. He felt the helplessness of a powerful warrior confronted with a situation where physical skill was not enough. But he found some comfort in the thought that, by now, Touch the Sky should be gone under—sent to his death by Wolf Who Hunts Smiling and Swift Canoe.

Again, his rage deep and black at the memory, he recalled his cousin and Swift Canoe swearing on the Sacred Arrows that Honey Eater was meeting with Touch the Sky in secret, that he was holding her in his blanket. He found it hard to accept, yet—they had sworn on the Arrows! His jealous rage had overcome even the Cheyenne dread of drawing tribal blood.

Before Honey Eater could reply, Arrow Keeper crossed to their tipi. Black Elk rose respectfully to greet their peace leader.

"The last word-bringers have returned to camp," he said. "All of the far-flung clans below the Platte River have been notified of the chief-renewal. I have decided the ceremony will be held in the middle of the Moon When the Cherries Ripen. It will take place near our old winter camp in the Tongue River valley."

Black Elk nodded at this important news.

Arrow Keeper pulled his blanket tighter around his shoulders. The old shaman's silver hair was still thick, his eyes sharp despite the leathery mask of wrinkles surrounding them.

"Have your cousin and Swift Canoe returned yet with a report on the Pawnee?"

Black Elk's eyes fled from his chief's. Arrow Keeper noted this. He had not been fooled when Black Elk, shortly after Touch the Sky rode out toward the Black Hills, had sent Touch the Sky's worst enemies on a "scouting mission."

"Not yet, Father," said Black Elk.

True, thought Arrow Keeper, River of Winds' report was damning and seemed to prove Touch the Sky was either a turncoat or at least a dog for the white men, cooperating in their treachery. But Arrow Keeper refused to believe appearances. And secretly, he knew Black Elk respected Touch the Sky too much to kill him like this, sullying the Arrows, without further proof.

No, thought the old shaman as he glanced at Honey Eater—here was the reason for Black Elk's shameful order. The girl was innocent, of course. But the Cheyenne way did not always allow for innocence.

"Perhaps," Arrow Keeper finally said, "your two young warriors have lost their way. Or perhaps they have met an enemy who fights better than they."

Both men understood the elder's hidden meaning. Arrow Keeper turned to leave. Then he turned back around and once again held Black Elk's eyes with his.

"If they do not return soon," he said, "Touch the Sky may arrive before them."

Hot blood crept into Black Elk's face. But he said nothing, holding his face impassive. Honey Eater stared at both men in turn, trying to read the real meaning of this strange conversation. Arrow Keeper watched Black Elk a few moments longer, disappointment keen in his eyes.

"Thankfully, Maiyun has His own battle plan," said the old shaman. "I have seen a vision and I will hold by it. What must be will be, and no mortal warrior can change this."

The next moment, like smoke caught on the wind, he was gone.

Chapter Fifteen

Near the spot where the Weeping Woman River oxbowed, Wolf Who Hunts Smiling and Swift Canoe rode into serious trouble.

The two Cheyenne youths had chosen this place to water their ponies. They were unaware that, recently, paleface miners had built a camp here. This followed the discovery of a modest amount of gold trapped in sediment pockets at the river's bend. The color had long since been exhausted by eager miners. But rumors and gold fever still drew dozens of desperate whites.

Now, bitter and frustrated, they welcomed the opportunity to grant a taste of vigilante justice to these marauding renegades.

The Cheyenne had topped a long rise and spotted the buckboards, canvas pyramid tents, and Indian-style tipis. White men swarmed like ants, and some of them spotted the two riders before they could retreat out of sight.

131

Judd Cole

"They will ride hard," said Wolf Who Hunts Smiling as a group of whites raced to mount up for the chase.

He had heard Black Elk and some of the Headmen speak of this thing. Soldiers of the Southern Dog Cheyenne had attacked and killed miners along the Platte. There were only a few of these Dog Soldiers, drunk on strong water and following the battle chief named War Horse. But white men needed only a few small acorns to conclude that a tall oak forest was in their way.

Wolf Who Hunts Smiling had been right—the white miners rode hard, dogging them like shadows. But their horses were fat from graining and lazy from prolonged grazing. Whites trained their horses for obedience, not endurance. They were good for short bursts of power and speed, not the sustained run.

Soon the iron bits of their mounts were flecked with foam. Meanwhile, the leaner, smaller, more spirited Indian ponies were opening the distance.

The miners abandoned the chase near sunset. The two Cheyenne found themselves in unfamiliar country, their ponies exhausted. The terrain was mostly hills covered with long Sudan grass, interspersed with jagged, red-dirt ravines.

They were skirting the steep bank of a dried-up creek when a startled fox bounded across their path.

Swift Canoe's paint, riding nearest to the creek, shied in fright and side-jumped. The left foreleg came down on clay and the bank crumbled, tumbling horse and rider down a steep decline to a dry, rock-strewn bed of hard-baked clay.

132

Even out of sight up above, Wolf Who Hunts Smiling heard the sickening noise when the pony landed head first, its neck snapping fast and clean. By the time he dismounted, calmed and hobbled his own pony, and climbed down, the paint was heaving—great, wracking death gasps. Bloody froth bubbled from its nostrils.

Swift Canoe had been thrown clear. But he was just now regaining consciousness. And his broken right arm lay at a ridiculously impossible angle to his body. Wolf Who Hunts Smiling winced when he saw a jagged stump of white bone protruding through a tear in the skin. It was a serious break. On the plains, it was a potentially deadly wound.

"Brother!"

Swift Canoe's strained voice hinted at the incredible pain. He had glanced at his pony, then his wound, and lost the color in his face.

"Look here! My pony is dead! And my arm! Brother, help me, I fear I am gone under!"

Swift Canoe's fear of dying showed now in his eyes. Wolf Who Hunts Smiling felt his face twist in disapproval. This was a bad situation, truly. But he was of the Panther Clan, as was his cousin Black Elk. The men of that clan placed high honor on never showing fear in their voice or face.

"Any good warrior may find himself upon the ground helpless," said Wolf Who Hunts Smiling. "There is no shame in this. But you are a bull, not a cow! Do not whine like a woman. Are we not both Cheyenne? Do we not take care of our own? Cease this talk of fear and death!"

But his words were wasted—Swift Canoe no longer heard him. The pain had washed over him in ever-increasing waves until numb shock took

133

over. He lay with his eyes wide-open but glazed, unseeing, while his teeth chattered like an elk-tooth necklace.

Wolf Who Hunts Smiling considered: Swift Canoe's Wolverine Clan were complainers and shirkers, true. Their women were notorious for hiding their meat rations, after a hunt distribution, and then lining up for a second allotment. But Swift Canoe, while certainly no battle leader, had counted coup and taken scalps like a man.

Besides—he was a loyal follower, and Wolf Who Hunts Smiling needed loyal followers. He was even more ambitious than his cousin Black Elk. He was not content, as Black Elk was, to serve as a war chief who ruled only in battle. He wanted to head his own band. He would lead the fight to drive the white dogs from the peaks and valleys and plains of the Shaiyena homeland.

For this, he would need loyal followers like Swift Canoe. Like Black Elk, Wolf Who Hunts Smiling was covered with hard bark. But he was also wily like his name—he must try to save Swift Canoe.

He thought about a travois. But what would he construct it from out here on the plains, no trees in sight? Besides, that would be too much weight for even his sturdy black, across such a distance.

Leaving him now and riding for help was also a bad plan. Wolf Who Hunts Smiling was not even sure where they were, nor how many sleeps it would require to find the tribe. The only sensible choice was to remain with him. He would tend to the wound and slaughter the dead pony so they would have meat—albeit raw meat, since they lacked wood for a fire. When Swift Canoe was able to survive on his own, Wolf Who Hunts

Smiling could then return to camp and send help back for him.

He was worried, though. True, they had shaken the white miners for good. But they had made no effort to cover their trail when they fled from Medicine Lake. What if the sharp-eyed Pawnee picked up on their sign?

Wolf Who Hunts Smiling thought of the Colt Model 1855 rifle in his buckskin scabbard above. He had plenty of bullets and percussion caps since the tribe had begun exchanging the season's beaver plews at the trading post in Red Shale. If lice-eaters attacked, he was at least in a good defensive position: open country in front of him, a deep creek bed behind him. He would sell his Cheyenne scalp dearly.

Thinking of the Pawnee made him also think of Woman Face. By now his enemy should be either dead or dying.

Swift Canoe groaned, begging for water.

Dead or dying, Wolf Who Hunts Smiling told himself again as he climbed the steep bank, struggling for hand- and footholds, back up to his pony and the bladder-bag of water. But by now he had begun to wonder if the rumors about Touch the Sky could possibly be true.

The rumors about strong medicine guiding his fate and protecting him.

Eluding the angry silvertip was only one of many times when the tall stranger had knocked Death from his pony before the Black Warrior could count first coup on his mortal soul. Wolf Who Hunts Smiling hated him. What right did he have, riding into a Cheyenne camp with the stink of murdering whites all over him? He drank strong water with

135

---

whites, he laid secret plans with them, he left talking papers for their Bluecoat pony soldiers in the hollows of trees. He even held one of their yellow-haired squaws in his blanket and made love talk! Besides— clearly Arrow Keeper had great plans for this tall stranger. Plans that Wolf Who Hunts Smiling's ambition would not abide.

This two-faced, many-tongued interloper deserved whatever fate the Pawnee had chosen for him. But now, as he climbed over the bank and stared out across the rolling plains, Wolf Who Hunts Smiling felt it again: the nagging suspicion that, in spite of everything, he would face his enemy again.

His cousin, the lake, lay calm and still when Touch the Sky finally began the ordeal of invoking a medicine dream.

He had no fear of the Pawnee returning soon. Much time had to pass before any lice-eater would visit an area known for bad medicine. They would face bullet or blade bravely. But at the first hint of enemy magic, they showed the white feather.

He had rested through the night, preparing for this day. To supplement his supply of venison, he had killed a plump rabbit and enjoyed his first taste of fresh meat in many sleeps. Now the wound in his side was merely a dull ache, like a bad memory blunted by time.

Though he rested well that night, sleep eluded him for a long time. He found his mind carefully considering the question of red man's medicine, the Indian's way of dealing with the supernatural. Some of the stories the elders told were foolish, of course. No Cheyenne believed all of them. But had he not seen proof of Arrow Keeper's big medicine?

Vision Quest

There was the time when Pawnee attacked Yellow Bear's camp. Touch the Sky had watched a lice-eater fire point-blank at Honey Eater, twice. But Arrow Keeper had thrown his magic panther skin over her just before the warrior fired, and the bullets went wide. And once Arrow Keeper had blessed Touch the Sky's horse with power, speed, and endurance—had the dun not flown like a fierce wind across the plains, easily catching the whiskey trader Henri Lagace on his magnificent cavalry sorrel?

Before his sister the sun rose for the day, Touch the Sky built a huge fire beside the lake. With the eerie tongues of orange flame casting his shadow against the trees, he began the rhythmic dancing that helped an Indian focus his mind. He moved in a wide, loose circle about the fire. He rattled stones wrapped in soft bark and lifted his knees high to the steady cadence of "Hi-ya, hi-ya!" His mind began to grow quiet; intrusive thoughts drifted into a fog that blew away.

With the first rays of dawn, Touch the Sky stripped naked. He touched his medicine bundle one last time, drawing strength from the badger claws within. Then he took his place atop a lone hill at one end of the lake. While sandpipers and other small shore birds stared at him curiously, he stood silent and stone still.

The dancing had already prepared him for the trance state which must happen if he were to endure the upcoming ordeal. He felt it coming on, a gradual but steady shutting down of the body as it moved into a state almost like hibernation. His muscles grew heavy and slack as they lost all unnecessary tension. His mind was clear, totally aware, not lost in the past or the future but existing now in the becoming that was the gateway to visions.

He stopped fighting the pain and discomfort, lost his fear, felt no hatred or jealousy or envy. Time and place became a river, flowing all around him, at first, then carrying him with the current.

He stared, unblinking, into the sun now, feeling no pain, doing no damage to his eyes. Gradually, as she tracked higher across the blue dome of the sky, his head tilted to follow her. His shadow was long behind him, grew short, now stretched out longer again in front of him as the sun finally eased toward her resting place. But the Cheyenne felt no sense of time passing, no reminder that he was rooted to the earth.

And then, at some point, he simply blinked once, and he was aware again in the usual way.

His body felt stiff, and the location of the Grandmother Star told him the night was well along. The air felt chilly, a harsh wind blew steadily from the north. But without debating it, Touch the Sky walked down to the lake and waded in.

The water was torturously cold against his sunbaked skin. But he kept moving out until the water reached his chin. Then, again, he untethered his mind from its usual awareness, freeing it from the little day and letting it seek the Vision Way.

Arrow Keeper had once told him how most people misunderstand visions. They assumed that visions came easily to the sick, sad, and dying because they were weak in their minds. They were not weak, Arrow Keeper insisted, they were *ready*.

And now, after his long ordeal on the plains, the dancing, his long day staring into the sun—

Touch the Sky too was ready.

First came the voices. But not dead voices from a dead past. Living voices guiding him now, here, on the upward path known as the medicine dream.

Old Knobby, the hostler at the feed stable in Bighorn Falls: *The Injun figgers he belongs to the land. The white man figgers the land belongs to him. They ain't meant to live together.*

John Hanchon, his white father: *I've worked until I'm mule-tired, but I still go to bed scared every night.*

He heard more voices, his mother and his friend Corey Robinson and Kristen Steele and the brevet officer Tom Riley and Little Horse and Honey Eater. And he felt no fear when the ghosts of the dead paraded past—Chief Yellow Bear, High Forehead, True Son, all trying to warn him, trying to tell him something. But he couldn't quite make out the words.

And then words gave way to sounds and mind pictures. He saw horses rearing, their eyes huge with fright, while red warriors sang their battle cry. Rivers of blood flowed everywhere, cannons roared, steel clashed against steel. From across the vast plains red warriors streamed, flowing like the blood they must soon shed. One brave led them, his war bonnet streaming coup feathers. But Touch the Sky could not see his face.

He saw glimpses of the ice-shrouded lands to the north. He saw the faces of his enemies, Hiram Steele and Seth Carlson. He saw a long ragged column of starving Cheyenne, again being led by the mysterious brave whose face he could not see.

Then, once again, he blinked, and he was aware of everything around him. Aware in the little day. But it was as if the night had been painted in brilliant hues, glazed in ceramic.

Overhead, the same eagle that had guided him here now circled gracefully, a ghostly silhouette in the moonlight. On shore, watching him with intent curiosity, was the huge grizzly. Only, now it showed no anger. It simply watched him with open curiosity. The moonlit lake shimmered like black ice, the eerie cries of the loons seemed to extend, distort, now grow distant and low, now shrill and close in his ears.

When the voice of Chief Yellow Bear came again, high, clear, right in his ears, Touch the Sky felt no fear.

"We who have crossed over," said this voice from the Land of Ghosts, "know everything that will pass. I have seen you bounce your son on your knee, just as I have seen you shed blood for that son and his mother.

"Touch the Sky, place these words close to your heart forever, for they will save the Shaiyena nation: *When all seems lost, become your enemy!*"

The voice faded, the mind pictures returned, and now Touch the Sky again saw the mysterious warrior leading his people. Only this time the war leader turned for a moment to look back, the war cry on his lips, and he recognized himself.

Touch the Sky wasn't sure how much longer he stood rooted in the frigid lake. But at some point he became aware that his teeth were chattering, his muscles cramped with cold. Stiff muscles protesting, he waded back to shore. As he stepped up out of the water, he spotted the eagle one last time:

It completed one full circle of the lake, then headed out across the plains.

He walked back to his clothing. Then, as he reached down for his clout, he froze.

Nestled atop his leggings was the object of his second vision during the journey here, the symbol of courage and fighting spirit in battle: an eagle-tail feather. He touched it—it was still warm from the eagle's body heat.

Only now, as the numbness in his body finally wore off, did the full significance of his medicine dream sink through to Touch the Sky.

There was no longer any question of it. Arrow Keeper was right. The hand of the Great Spirit was indeed involved in this thing. He could not be sure of the meaning of everything he saw. Image had piled upon image, sound blended with sound, and the events of many years seemed telescoped into the intensity of a moment.

But Arrow Keeper was right. His arrival at Yellow Bear's tribe was not some random happening. That birthmark hidden behind his hair—it was not some random marking. Touch the Sky could not be sure of his part, but Fate had already written a role for him. A great role, but one with many great responsibilities and hardships.

Touch the Sky understood and accepted all this. Just as, once and for all, he accepted his destiny as a Cheyenne. Holding the feather in one hand, he vowed to return and face his tribe again no matter what.

Chapter Sixteen

"It is as I feared," said Wolf Who Hunts Smiling. "The lice-eaters were not content with killing Woman Face. They followed our sign, and now the fight comes to us."

The sun glowed straight overhead out of a cloudless sky. But even squinting, Wolf Who Hunts Smiling could see the group of riders approaching straight toward them. They had stopped, one of them dismounting and kneeling to the ground— clearly he was reading sign.

The Cheyenne's horse was picketed below in the creek bed. Wolf Who Hunts Smiling had used their two buffalo robes and a few arrow shafts to rig a small shelter from the sun. Swift Canoe lay inside it now, sweltering in the breezeless heat.

"Brother, my arm is useless," Swift Canoe called up to him, "or I would join you. You can kill me now and ride hard and perhaps outrun them."

In fact Wolf Who Hunts Smiling had already considered this plan. But it was too late now. The night before he had dug for a long time in the creek bed, finally discovering a thin layer of alkali-tasting water. If he rode out now, in this unfamiliar country, when would he next reach water?

Besides—these were Indian ponies, not the lazy plugs ridden by whites. He would never stand a chance of outrunning the Pawnee.

No, he was safest right here. Let his enemy come at him. They had no shelter for a hidden attack. He would pick them off like prairie chickens, well protected in his natural breastwork of the creek bed. His pony was safe below.

Again he carefully inspected his bullets and primer caps in the soft kid pouch at his elbow. A grain of sand could clog up the Colt's firing mechanism.

"I have no ears for this talk of killing each other," he said to Swift Canoe. "I plan to grease Pawnee bones with war paint! One bullet, one enemy."

"*This* is the he-bear talk!" said Swift Canoe. "We are the fighting Cheyenne!"

"If the fight goes bad and they send me under," said Wolf Who Hunts Smiling, "remember that you have your knife and one good arm—sing the Death Song and fall on your own blade. You do not want to be captured by lice-eaters."

But his warning was unnecessary. Swift Canoe, like all Cheyenne warriors, lived in dread of Pawnee torture. His knife was already in his hand.

By now the riders were almost in long-arm range. Wolf Who Hunts Smiling inserted a primer cap into the loading gate of the Colt. He had no intention of waiting until the Pawnee were close enough to discover them. His hope was to keep them back out of rifle range.

And to pray to Maiyun for a full moon and a starlit night. The Pawnee were in their element after dark.

He sighted on one of the riders, ignoring the smaller target presented by the brave and aiming instead for the middle of his pony's chest. He inserted his finger inside the trigger guard and slowly took up the slack.

Red Plume signaled a halt while Gun Powder dismounted and examined the ground for signs.

"The white men quit chasing them some time back," reported the Pawnee scout. "They slowed their mounts—the tracks are closer together and not so deep. Now they are riding easy."

Red Plume nodded. "Then we should catch them soon. This is not Indian territory and they will be lost. Be they Sioux or Cheyenne, *this* time we take prisoners. By now the Cheyenne tribe has decided on a time and place for their chief-renewal. A Sioux will know this thing as well as his cousin the Cheyenne."

"The riders are Cheyenne or Sioux," agreed Gun Powder. "Crow ponies have a cleft hoof. The Arapaho and Shoshone have both traveled toward the Land of the Grandmother to the north, following the buffalo herds. We are too far south for these to be the prints of Mandan or Hidatsa."

"And you are sure the trail started at Medicine Lake?"

Gun Powder nodded. "Near the same time as we arrived. The dirt is still not crusted in the tracks."

"This means they played the rabbit when they spotted us. I suspect these two are word-bringers. No doubt they had a message for the bear-calling shaman."

Red Plume had lost enough face when the Cheyenne youth with the powerful medicine had sent him scrambling with the rest of his braves, fleeing like children afraid of the Wendigo. Now they had exhausted one full sleep in an impromptu council, debating whether or not to follow this trail. This time it would be different. This time the men of men would demonstrate why they were the most feared warriors in all the Plains Indian country.

Before he could give the order to ride, however, Short Buffalo spoke up. Though his words were still muffled and indistinct because of the wounds to his mouth, this time no one laughed. His words were too serious.

"Brothers! Hear me! You know me. We have hunted and traveled the war path together, and visited as friends in our clan lodges. You know my clan, and you know my society!"

Absolute silence followed this. Every brave present knew that Short Buffalo was a member of the Death Arrow Society, a Pawnee military society which attracted only the most courageous—but also only the most reckless—of warriors. Each member of the Death Arrows carried a black-painted arrow always in his quiver. That arrow could never be drawn save on one condition: that it must draw blood. If the brave failed to kill his enemy with it, then he was required by the society's law to kill himself in expiation.

Every buck present, including Red Plume,

knew the significance of his action when Short Buffalo now slid the black arrow from his quiver. By that action he had pledged his life for the rare honor of overriding normal tribal law or even the commands of his war leader. Red Plume was bound by the manly heroism of such an act: Short Buffalo had sworn to kill, and he would be allowed to do so on his own terms. Failing this, he must die.

Every brave present was inspired by Short Buffalo's act.

"Mount!" Red Plume commanded Gun Powder. "Now we teach our ponies about hard riding!"

He sounded the shrill Pawnee war yip, and the rest of the braves repeated it. They dug heels and knees into their ponies, urging them to a hard run. Their greased topknots gleamed in the stark sunlight, and several had streaked their nearly naked bodies with vermillion dye.

Short Buffalo raced out ahead of them, his war lance held high. No one heard a shot nor detected a puff of muzzle smoke. But a moment later, a piebald pony next to Short Buffalo collapsed as if its bones had turned to water.

Touch the Sky had made good time during the first morning after he left Medicine Lake, bearing due west toward the Cheyenne camp at the fork where the Powder River joined the Little Powder. But a Bluecoat cavalry patrol ambushed him near Beaver Creek and flushed him far into the even more desolate terrain of the southern country.

The solders gave up past midday. His horse was well rested and fed, and Touch the Sky had filled his sash with fruits and nuts to supplement the rest of his venison. This delay in unfamiliar country seemed a trifling thing now after all he had endured.

Then, toward sundown, he heard the first shots.

They came at regular intervals, as if one person were firing and reloading, firing and reloading, using cool battlefield discipline. A long pause, the thunder of hooves, another interval of regularly spaced shots.

A series of red dirt ravines pockmarked the area. Touch the Sky was able to stick mostly to the cover of these as he slipped closer. Finally he emerged from one and cautiously peered out from behind a long, low, grass-covered hummock.

The sight sent blood throbbing into his face. It was the same group of Pawnee who had planned to kill him back at Medicine Lake!

From his present location, Touch the Sky could not see whoever it was they were engaging in a harassment attack. Two ponies lay dead on the ground, a third kicked in death agonies. One Pawnee lay still, apparently dead, another bled from a wound in his arm. They were grouped behind the war leader called Red Plume. Evidently they had retreated to a spot just out of the defender's effective range.

Even as Touch the Sky watched, a brave dug heels into his pony and rode out from the group. He raced in a zig-zagging pattern toward what Touch the Sky now recognized as a creek, the lip of its bank barely visible from where he watched.

The rifle spoke its piece, the Pawnee charged on, still swerving and doubling back across his own path on his surefooted pony.

Another shot, another miss. The pony raced closer.

A third shot, and the pony was down. Almost without missing a beat, the agile rider raced on foot back toward his companions. A final shot kicked up a yellow plume of dust at his retreating heels.

Touch the Sky wondered who was under siege. It sounded like a lone fighter, unless his companions had been killed or injured. No white settlers or Bluecoats would travel alone out here. It was almost surely a red man. With the exception of the Ute tribe, any enemy of the Pawnee was a friend of the Cheyenne. And Touch the Sky knew no mountain-dwelling Ute would be in this area.

He studied the lay of the land and tried to guess in what direction that creek might twist and wind. Then, sticking to the jagged ravines and hiding behind hummocks, he went in search of it.

He found it without much trouble while the sun still gave light. Touch the Sky hobbled his pony and proceeded along the dried, baked-clay bed cautiously. He heard several more shots, the sound drawing near as he advanced.

His heart raced faster as he approached a sharp bend, close now to the sounds of rifle shots. He rounded it slowly, hugging the steep bank and staying in its apron of shade.

For a moment his head denied his eyes when he recognized Wolf Who Hunts Smiling dug in at the top of the bank. He was sighting out toward the Pawnee with the Colt that had once belonged to Touch the Sky. Below, his anxious face protruding from a crude hide shelter-half, was Swift Canoe.

148

Swift Canoe clutched his bone-handle knife in his hand.

"Brother!" Wolf Who Hunts Smiling called down to him. "I fear it will soon go badly for us. I think the lice-eaters are finally tired of being picked off like nits from a buffalo! They are massing for the charge! Let them come, I am for them! But only this, brother: If they should hit me and only wound me, do not fall on your knife until you have made sure I am gone over. Do not leave me for them to take alive."

"I swear this thing, Cheyenne warrior," Swift Canoe promised.

Touch the Sky did not stop to wonder why the two Cheyenne were marooned this far from the Powder River camp. Nor why their path had crossed that of the same Pawnee with whom he'd tangled. Their courage, in the face of such a dire threat, impressed him.

He hated both of them. And both had tried to kill him. But they were behaving like true warriors now, and were they not Cheyenne? His battle with them was a battle within the tribe—this was an enemy from without, one who attacked in darkness and killed women and children while they slept in their robes.

He could not just let them die. Nor would it save any of them if he joined the fight beside Wolf Who Hunts Smiling. There were still a half-dozen good braves thirsty for blood. This was not a time for fighting.

Touch the Sky climbed to the top of the bank and carefully peered out, getting his bearing. Then he dropped back down and followed his back-trail, heading toward a nearby ravine.

* * *

"It is settled," said Red Plume. "Short Buffalo has spoken and I have spoken. He will ride in alone. We follow. He draws first blood or dies. But we have waited long enough. I care not if Mother Night would protect us, I am for blood now! We attack now, as one!"

Short Buffalo was tired of words. His horse leaped out from the others and raced toward the creek. It was a roan mare, trained to turn buffalo herds and nimble on its feet. Short Buffalo borrowed a trick from the Cheyenne and rode low hugging his pony's neck to make a small target.

The agile pony leaped over one dead horse, another, swerved right, left, swept past the dead Pawnee. One shot missed. A second dropped the roan and its rider when they were less than a stone's throw away from the creek.

Unlike his comrades, Short Buffalo did not retreat out of range. He sounded the war yip and raced into the teeth of his enemy.

Desperate but moving with calm competence, Wolf Who Hunts Smiling loaded one of his last bullets and primer caps. He waited until the enraged Pawnee was blocking the sun, then squeezed the trigger.

There was a brief sizzling sound when the primer cap misfired.

"Sing the Death Song!" shouted Wolf Who Hunts Smiling to Swift Canoe even as he frantically clawed his own knife out of its sheath.

Short Buffalo leaped, thrusting his stone-tipped lance at Wolf Who Hunts Smiling. The small but quick and strong Cheyenne lunged to one side and avoided the lance. At the same moment, he brought his knife up to meet Short Buffalo.

The Pawnee impaled himself and tumbled into the creek, his war cry transformed into a death shriek. But the impact had knocked Wolf Who Hunts Smiling down too. And above, he and Swift Canoe could hear the rest of the attackers thundering closer.

Deciding it was better to die above fighting, instead of trapped down there like a cowering child, Wolf Who Hunts Smiling climbed back over the bank.

Just as he emerged, a furious bellow from his right drew everyone's attention.

Wolf Who Hunts Smiling's jaw dropped open in astonishment when Touch the Sky—not even armed—emerged from a ravine and ran straight at the Pawnee. The ridiculous fool was woofing and growling like a silvertip bear, as if that should somehow frighten blood-lusting Pawnee warriors! Had he gone Wendigo?

But his astonishment turned to pure shock moments later, when the Pawnee showed the white feather and tore off across the plains!

Red Plume knew the Pawnee nations were in trouble now. See how this mysterious, bear-summoning Cheyenne shaman arrived out of thin air to protect his own? Until they knew more about him and his powerful medicine, Red Plume knew he must recommend to the council that all plans for attacking the Cheyenne chief-renewal be canceled.

Chapter Seventeen

The Pawnee were soon mere dust devils on the horizon. Wolf Who Hunts Smiling stared at his tribal enemy as he crossed closer toward the creek.

A sudden thought weakened his knees: Where was Woman Face's horse, his weapons? How could he simply have appeared out of the earth like a thing of smoke?

How, wondered Wolf Who Hunts Smiling, unless this was not Touch the Sky but his ghost?

All in an instant, it made horrible but logical sense. The Pawnee *had* tortured and killed him! Why else would they have fled, the very first moment they spotted him, like dogs with their tails on fire?

It also made gruesome sense that Touch the Sky's ghost would now imitate the silvertip. Was this not the animal his Cheyenne enemies lured to kill him? To Wolf Who Hunts Smiling, as to most

Indians, ghosts who return to the body-world are revenants—spirits bent on revenge.

Thinking these things, Wolf Who Hunts Smiling forgot his recent stern lecture to Swift Canoe about courage under pressure. He also violated the manly code of his Panther Clan: Fear turned his face white, his eyes huge. His lips trembled as if he had suddenly been thrown naked into a snowbank. Clearly, he wore his terror in his face.

"Leave this place!" he said in his bewilderment.

He made the cut-off sign even though he knew such mild white magic was useless against a spirit manifestation.

Touch the Sky, now totally bewildered himself, stopped. He stood perhaps 20 paces back from the bank of the dried-up creek. Wolf Who Hunts Smiling had hollowed out a crude rifle pit. Only the upper part of his body was visible. Now and then a frustrated Swift Canoe called up to him, desperate to learn what was going on. Wolf Who Hunts Smiling ignored him, busy fending off complete panic.

"I fought with you, I drew your blood," said Wolf Who Hunts Smiling. "And true it is I walked between you and the fire. But I never crept up on you from behind like a cowardly Mandan or came for you in your sleep like the treacherous Comanche! When you were trapped in the whiskey traders' camp, I fought like ten warriors to free you. True, I wanted to kill you. But in a fair fight, warrior to warrior!"

This talk amazed Touch the Sky. He watched Wolf Who Hunts Smiling again make the cut-off sign. Clearly his enemy was convinced beyond all doubt he had returned from the Land of Ghosts.

153

But why did he think this thing? What could have convinced him he had been killed?

Then, a heartbeat later, he understood.

He understood everything.

Now it was clear to him what these two Cheyenne—his sworn enemies—were doing in this desolate no-man's-land so far from camp. *Now* he understood why that grizzly had so suddenly shown up at an uninhabited cave. He also knew how that freshly blooded fawn had gotten there.

It was bait planted by Wolf Who Hunts Smiling and Swift Canoe. Bait intended to lure his executioner.

His anger was tempered by his private amusement as Touch the Sky grasped the situation. For the first time in his memory, Wolf Who Hunts Smiling had lost his arrogant, wily sneer. Why not enjoy this rare turn of events?

"You say you only wanted to kill me in a fair fight. Then tell me, Cheyenne buck. Would *you* face a silvertip bear and call it a fair fight?"

Wolf Who Hunts Smiling was shamed into silence.

"And speak of this thing, great warrior. The night, at the white dogs' camp on the Yellowstone, when you threw rocks to alert the paleface sentry? You ran away and left me to die. Was this another time when you wanted me to die in a 'fair fight'?"

"These—these things were wrong," admitted Wolf Who Hunts Smiling. "But River of Winds has recently sworn that he saw you making medicine with Bluecoats! And that time with the sentry, I was still angry after our fight which caused

Black Elk to turn against me.

"But you were *not* killed as the result of anything I did, each time I left you a fighting chance. This is not the same as murder!"

"A long, thin creature that slides on the ground and bites me with poison is the same as a snake to me," said Touch the Sky. "Call it whatever else you will. When you speak this way, you mangle words. Just like the white men who write talking papers and then steal our land with them. They call a white rock black when it suits their purpose, just as you now honey-coat your treachery."

"Kill me if you will," said Wolf Who Hunts Smiling. "Show me the Wendigo's face and turn me to frozen stone. But do not say I am anything like the white devils who slaughtered my father!"

"I say it again! Evil was not invented by the white man—I have seen red men who would make the white devil Satan proud indeed."

Wolf Who Hunts Smiling looked at the ground, knowing full well who he meant.

"What?" said Touch the Sky. "The child sulks! Will you now threaten to kill me again? It was your favorite sport while I walked the earth."

"I have ears for this," said Wolf Who Hunts Smiling. "You are right to mock me now. I spoke of it too much. Women fight with their words, men let their battle lances speak for them."

Touch the Sky permitted his lips to widen in a wry smile.

"Are you telling me, then, that now you wish you would have killed me quickly and been done with it long ago?"

Wolf Who Hunts Smiling looked like a fox caught in a blind trap. He hadn't meant to reveal

so much of his true thoughts. Yet, it was foolish to lie to a ghost—it was said by the elders
they could read the human heart the way living
Indians could read a game trail.

Fear drained even the wily gleam from Wolf
Who Hunts Smiling's eyes. But courageously, he
nodded. "I wish now that *I* had sent you under,
not Pawnee."

Touch the Sky could not help admiring his
enemy's audacious courage even as he loathed
him for his petty hatred and jealousy and ambition. Abruptly, he reached down, picked up a
handful of dirt, and let it scatter in the wind.

"Tell me, Panther Clan!" he said to Wolf Who
Hunts Smiling, each word laced with scorn.
"How can a thing of smoke move the dirt—let
alone harm a brave warrior such as yourself?"

It took Wolf Who Hunts Smiling many heartbeats to understand his mistake. When he realized, blood rushed into his face. Humiliation
vied with rage and relief. Reflexively, he raised
the Colt and aimed it at Touch the Sky. For a long
moment the two Cheyenne stared at each other,
faces carved from stone, eyes unwavering.

Then Wolf Who Hunts Smiling lowered the Colt.
"Enjoy your white man's joke. What happened here
this day," he said coldly, pointing out toward the
battlefield where dead ponies and dead Pawnee
still lay, "showed once again your great courage.
You know I hate you, yet you saved me."

"I saved a Cheyenne," Touch the Sky corrected
him.

"As you say. I *still* believe you secretly play the
dog for whites. But I see now that I was wrong
about your loyalty to the tribe. A Cheyenne who

risks his life for a tribe member he hates will surely stand and cover himself with glory for those he loves.

"Even so, I feel it in my bones, the day comes when we will tip our lances at each other. And I *will* kill you—honorably or otherwise—if I obtain proof with my own eyes that you serve the Long Knives against us. Until such a day arrives, I swear this thing on my medicine bag: Never again will I sully the Arrows by deliberately endangering you in secret as I have done in the past."

"I play the dog for no one," said Touch the Sky. "But I have placed your words in my sash. I fear they are as close to a truce as we will ever come." Touch the Sky recalled his medicine dream at the lake and added, "I too feel we will one day meet in combat. One of us will sully the Arrows by killing a Cheyenne."

Wolf Who Hunts Smiling nodded. "I will wait here with Swift Canoe. Will you tell them back at camp where to find us?"

Touch the Sky nodded. "And I will mark the trail clearly with sign so they will be quick getting here."

Touch the Sky had taken several steps back toward his hidden pony when the other Cheyenne called his name. He turned around.

Wolf Who Hunts Smiling brandished the Colt rifle.

"You have long wanted your weapon back. I offer it freely now."

Touch the Sky debated. Black Elk had already taken the percussion-action Sharps rifle his white father had given him. He couldn't be trusted with it, Black Elk explained, after the report from River of Winds. Why, thought Touch the Sky now, give Black Elk a second weapon to steal? He was riding back to enough trouble and hostility as it was. Approaching camp now with a long arm might even get him killed.

"You turned it into a true firestick this day," Touch the Sky finally said. "I quit claim to it. The rifle is yours."

"I accept it gladly!" Wolf Who Hunts Smiling called to his retreating back. "Just carry my warning close to your heart. I respect you, yes. But I respect *any* enemy who is worth the effort of killing!"

Chapter Eighteen

When he arrived at the rim of the fertile Powder
River valley, Touch the Sky halted his pony.

The day was late, and the sun burned low on
the western horizon. Far below he could see the
Cheyenne camp. The tipis were arranged by clan
circle with a huge clearing left open in the center. It was dominated by the largest structure, the
hide-covered council lodge. Naked children played
at war, riding stick ponies into battle and carrying willow-branch shields. Squaws bent over their
cooking tripods to prepare the late meal.

Touch the Sky knew that sentries were posted
beyond this point, covering the approach to camp.
But something else had begun troubling him as he
neared the valley: What if there was now an order
to kill him on sight?

After all, he had left camp with most believing he
was a spy for the Long Knives. True, Arrow Keep-

er's power as acting chief was enough to permit his departure. But even Arrow Keeper had warned him to leave right away, during the night—as if afraid the tribe might override him. A chief was bound by the collective will of the tribe. Anything might have happened since he left.

Since his epic vision at Medicine Lake, Touch the Sky wanted more than ever to belong to the tribe, to be accepted. The prospect of being killed on sight did not trouble him because he was afraid, or because the thought of death held a sting for him as for all men. Rather, he did not want to die alone. He did not want to pass through this life on earth belonging nowhere, treated like a rabid cur by white and red men alike.

To belong just once before he died! And for this he had decided once and for all to make his stand in life as a Cheyenne, the blood of his birthright and as good a birthright as any man's. Several sleeps earlier, he would gladly have ridden into a sentry's arrow and ended this eternal fight just to survive.

Now, however, he decided he wanted to live, to explore the full length of his tether before he crossed over to the Land of Ghosts. So he would wait until his sister the sun went to her rest. Then he would slip past the sentries and simply throw himself on Arrow Keeper's mercy.

While he waited, watching the valley slide further into shadows, he picked out Black Elk's tipi. This was simple, for it was easily the finest and newest in the entire camp, and the meat racks behind overflowing. But the entrance flap remained closed. He failed to catch even a glimpse of Honey Eater.

Angry at himself, he forced his eyes away. Yes, he would make his stand with the Cheyenne, if he could. But Honey Eater was smoke behind him now, part of a world that was dead to him. She belonged to a time when hopes for love still lived in his heart. That time was gone. She was married now, another man's wife.

Chief Yellow Bear's words from the recent vision came back to him, a memory echo that pimpled his skin with gooseflesh:

I have seen you bounce your son on your knee, just as I have seen you shed blood for that son and his mother.

But who would his bride be, then? He had no room in his heart for any woman but Honey Eater.

While he thought these things, the sun slid lower and the first stars began to wink high in the night sky. Touch the Sky waited until the valley was shrouded in a cloak of black velvet darkness. Then, leading the gray by her hackamore, he carefully descended into the valley.

He was forced to swing wide, at one point, to avoid a sentry camped on a ridge above the eastern entrance to the Cheyenne village. And Touch the Sky worried, as he reached the edge of the camp clearing, about setting the dogs off: The Cheyenne kept many dogs around, training them to hate the smell of their enemies. But they could also go into a barking frenzy at the arrival of a Cheyenne.

But they ignored him as he slipped out of the trees. Touch the Sky skirted the tipis and the light from the huge fires in front of the lodges of the clans and military societies. First he turned his pony loose in the huge rope corral beside the river. Then, heart hammering against his ribs, he made his way toward Arrow Keeper's tipi.

It stood on a lone hummock between the river and the clan circles. The flap was up, a small fire burned within. The hide tipi cover had stretched so thin that the firelight inside turned it a soft orange-yellow color that glowed like burning punk. The old shaman's hatchet-sharp profile stood out clearly in silhouette.

Touch the Sky glanced inside. Arrow Keeper sat with his back to the entrance, silver-streaked hair spilling over his blanket-draped shoulders.

Touch the Sky looked closer, and a reverent awe filled him: Arrow Keeper held one of the sacred Cheyenne Medicine Arrows. Carefully, lovingly, he brushed its entire blue-and-yellow-striped length with a soft piece of chamois.

Touch the Sky was about to announce his presence. Suddenly, his back still turned, Arrow Keeper's gravelly voice said, "Welcome, Touch the Sky. Step inside and visit with your chief."

The old shaman turned around now. His nut-brown face was sere and wrinkled. But his eyes blazed with the intensity of the spirit flame that stays strong even when the body sickens and ages.

"I knew you were coming," he said as the youth stepped inside. "A great eagle circled camp this morning. It dropped this in front of my tipi."

The medicine man held up the tail feather of an eagle.

Touch the Sky felt his blood singing as he stared at the feather.

"I have one just like it, Father."

The shaman nodded. He slipped the Medicine Arrow back into the coyote fur pouch which held the other three Arrows. Arrow Keeper slid the pouch under his sleeping robes.

"Tell me, little brother," he said. "Did you find the vision you sought?"

Touch the Sky nodded. "It was as you said. Much was not clear, and already I have forgotten some things. But Father, this I know, my place is here with the tribe. Will they accept me?"

Arrow Keeper was silent for many heartbeats.

"I cannot speak the will of the tribe," he finally answered. "I cannot assure you they will accept you, not quickly. River of Winds' report has branded you a spy, or at least a traitor, in the eyes of many. But I *can* assure you they will tolerate your presence. And then perhaps, with time, acceptance will come if you earn it."

"How can you assure this thing?"

"I have long considered something. Twice now you have experienced a medicine dream, this time at Medicine Lake and earlier, before you rode against the paleface merchants of strong water."

Touch the Sky said, "There were two others during my journey. Smaller visions."

Arrow Keeper nodded. "I have reached a decision."

Grunting with the effort, stiff kneecaps popping, Arrow Keeper rose and stepped outside into the night. Touch the Sky was curious when he heard the acting chief call a young boy over. Arrow Keeper said something and the boy raced off.

Shortly after, to Touch the Sky's astonishment,

Black Elk stepped into the tipi.

"You sent for me, Father?" he was saying as he entered. Then he spotted Touch the Sky, and his jaw slacked open.

"You!" He spoke before he could stop himself.

Arrow Keeper was enjoying himself immensely but kept his smile turned inward.

"Black Elk seems surprised," said Arrow Keeper. "Almost as though he were staring at a ghost."

Black Elk had recovered somewhat and regained his fierce aspect. His dark eyes snapped sparks in the soft light of the tipi. In spite of himself, Touch the Sky again found himself staring at Black Elk's dead lump of ear. The warrior himself had sewn it back onto his head with buckskin thread after a Bluecoat saber severed it.

"Not a ghost, Father," he said, "a turncoat spy who licks the hand of his white masters, then sniffs at our Cheyenne women!"

"So you say." Arrow Keeper looked at Touch the Sky. "Have you seen Wolf Who Hunts Smiling and Swift Canoe?" he asked with exaggerated innocence. "They have been gone ever since you left. No doubt our war chief must wonder where his best bucks are hiding."

Black Elk's discomfort was obvious. Now Touch the Sky understood—Black Elk had ordered his death.

"I have seen them," Touch the Sky replied. Briefly, withholding most of the details, he explained that Swift Canoe was hurt and where they could be found.

"Tell me this also," said Arrow Keeper, his sharp old eyes fastened on Black Elk. "Did they attempt to kill you?"

The silence inside the tipi grew tense. By Cheyenne law, what Black Elk had done—ordering the assassination of a fellow tribe member without decree of the Headmen—was a serious crime. Black Elk could be stripped of his coup feathers and his possessions, lose his position as war leader.

And thus, thought Touch the Sky, plunge Honey Eater into a destitute marriage. He could not do that.

Touch the Sky met Black Elk's eyes as he spoke. He recalled Wolf Who Hunts Smiling's careful distinction between murder and placing a life in danger.

"They did not lift a finger against me," he replied truthfully enough. "Their bloody battle was with the Pawnee."

Relief washed over Black Elk's face. Arrow Keeper studied Touch the Sky for a long time, then nodded. He understood this gesture: The youth was extending an offer of peace to Black Elk, and Arrow Keeper approved this.

But in his secret heart of hearts, Black Elk was implacable in his jealous hatred. This stinking dog had met secretly with his squaw—perhaps he even lifted her dress and bulled her! He could not speak this shame to the others, but neither could he let this outsider return so Honey Eater would see him. Her heart was already filled with thoughts of him as it was.

Arrow Keeper seemed to read much of this in his war chief's face. Now, his voice all authority and business, he said, "The Councillors meet soon. You will make the following announcement. As of this day, Touch the Sky has become my apprentice.

He is blessed with the gift of vision-seeking. Therefore I will teach him the arts of the medicine man."

Both Black Elk and Touch the Sky were stunned by this proclamation. Arrow Keeper was not only acting chief but the tribe's permanent medicine man. This double authority gave his decision the force of law. Touch the Sky's acceptance or rejection by the tribe meant little now—with this important decision, Arrow Keeper had ended all talk of banishment or execution.

"Your training will be hard," he said to Touch the Sky. "And long. There is much to learn, and a young man can quickly grow bored with it. But I am convinced Maiyun has marked you out for a shaman."

Touch the Sky nodded. He was still surprised but submitted humbly. Black Elk, however, started to protest.

"Father! Think on this thing. River of Winds—"

"River of Winds," Arrow Keeper interrupted him, "is a good, honest brave. But he has been deceived by appearances. This buck before you is straight-arrow Cheyenne!"

"But he—"

"Now my old ears can hear no more," said Arrow Keeper. "Your chief has spoken. Now leave, both of you, and let an old man smile in his dreams."

Touch the Sky left his possessions in his tipi. Most of the activity in camp was now centered around the various lodges and the common square, where the young men were gathering for the pony races. He avoided those places, walking down to the river to bathe.

By chance Little Horse had just returned to camp from a word-bringing mission. Arrow Keeper had sent him to Sun Dance's Lakota village to inform the Sioux of the place and time for the upcoming chief-renewal. Little Horse had led his pony to the river to drink. Touch the Sky spotted him and the two friends had joyously embraced.

Touch the Sky was still recounting the events of his remarkable journey to Medicine Lake as the two friends headed back toward Touch the Sky's tipi. Abruptly, Little Horse laid a hand on his friend's arm.

"Hold, brother," he said in a whisper.

He pointed toward Touch the Sky's tipi. Because he had no clan affiliation in this Northern Cheyenne band, Touch the Sky's tipi, like the chief's, stood by itself.

In a slanting shaft of pale silver moonlight directly in front of the tipi knelt Honey Eater. Touch the Sky felt his pulse quicken at this unexpected glimpse of her frail beauty.

Every evening when Touch the Sky was away from camp, Honey Eater added another ritual to her nightly habit of picking fresh columbine for her hair: She would also stop in front of his tipi to verify that the stone was still there—the stone which he had placed there as a symbol of his eternal love. When it melted, he had sworn to her, so too would his love for her.

Tonight, again, it was still there. Honey Eater knelt, picked up the smooth round piece of white marble. For a moment she pressed it to the chamois-soft skin over her heart. An involuntary sob hitched in her chest, escaped in a choking gasp. Teardrops formed on her eyelids, and she placed the stone back down, hurrying away.

Touch the Sky was left speechless for a long time, doubting what he had seen. Then, when he could deny it no longer, he looked at his friend.

"Did my eyes alone just see Honey Eater?"

Little Horse shook his head. "Brother, *this* was no vision! You are a true warrior and can read many signs. But you are slow to grasp what any jaybird could tell you. Honey Eater loves you strong and true. What we have just seen, this takes place each night you are gone from camp. She hides it well, but I have seen."

"Each night I am gone," repeated Touch the Sky in a dumb trance of joy. A tight bud of emotion locked deep inside him threatened to blossom.

"Believe it, Bear Caller! Have I ever talked more than one way to you? Brother, Honey Eater has placed herself at great risk to learn about you. She cries for you and starts up, hope burning in her eyes, every time a rider approaches camp."

These words were soothing balsam for the aching wound in his heart. Touch the Sky's throat swelled tight with emotion.

"Brother," said Little Horse, "perhaps it is wrong to fan your hopes now that Honey Eater wears the bride-shawl. But she loves you, not Black Elk! I am no gossip like the women who buzz around the sewing lodge. But I have heard a thing."

"If you are no gossiping woman, then do not play the coy one either. Speak of this thing."

"You know that my cousin, Long Sash, is a Bowstring?"

Touch the Sky nodded. The Bowstrings were one of the six Cheyenne military societies, open to warriors of any clan. Black Elk too was a Bowstring.

"Long Sash was visiting at their dance lodge when Black Elk showed up with blood in his eye. You know that Black Elk despises all talk of feelings. But Long Sash says Black Elk had been drinking corn beer with the Lakota. He spoke of cutting off Honey Eater's braids to shame her into doing her duty as his wife. He swore by the four directions that she *would* give him a son whether she chose to or not.

"Brother, is it not as plain as tracks in fresh mud? Honey Eater is not lying with her own husband. Do you think any woman can treat Black Elk this way and not suffer for it? Her heart is for you, buck!"

First Arrow Keeper, now Little Horse—both assuring him Honey Eater's heart belonged to him despite everything. And now Touch the Sky had seen the proof with his eyes. A woman in love with her husband would not be crying in front of another man's tipi!

Honey Eater loved him. Now he had the best reason of all for staying. Never mind that she was married to Black Elk. It was marriage in name only. Clearly, Black Elk's furious jealousy foretold great trouble for both of them. But so long as she loved him—so long as her body ached for his as he did for her—he would never let his hopes face anywhere but east.

"Brother," he said to Little Horse, "I am glad

you are my friend. But your loyalty will soon be sorely tested. This time I stay. I am a Cheyenne. Anyone who plans to drive me off must be ready to kill me or die."